Unbroken
Circle

by
Mary Griggs

Bella
BOOKS

2011

Bella Books, Inc.
P.O. Box 10543
Tallahassee, FL 32302

Printed in the United States of America on acid-free paper
First published 2011

Editor: Katherine V. Forrest
Cover Designer: Judy Fellows

ISBN 13: 978-1-59493-243-4

Acknowledgments

While writing may be a solitary pursuit, I owe the reality of this novel to a number of people.

Both my parents have been an immense support in every way. Despite all the trouble I got into growing up, they have kept open their home and their hearts for everything I've ever needed. They even provided the occasional kick in the butt to motivate me to realize my dream of becoming a published author. I especially want to thank my mom, Fran, for giving me my first book and teaching me to always make books (and the time to read) a priority in my life.

I would like to thank my courageous first readers for reviewing my initial attempts at novel writing. Jennie and Brian Brick offered suggestions for the story's improvement with enough humor and grace to nurture my budding aspirations. Charlotte Klasson copy-edited the manuscript in preparation for sending it around to publishers. She is also my official photographer. Allison Alsup read the manuscript after the first rejection and gave me terrific advice about additions and rewrites.

Marianne K. Martin helped me with some substantive edits, including the advice to get right into the action. While tossing out the first two chapters was painful, their removal was essential and I'm grateful the time she was able to spare in the midst of writing and promoting her own novel.

Special thanks to Karin Kallmaker for changing my mind about romances and for inspiring me to write my own. I also really appreciate that she made time at the Sixth Annual Golden

Crown Literary Conference to look over my proposal and sample chapter and that she liked what she saw well enough to request the entire manuscript for Bella Books. Receiving the acceptance call from her is one of the highlights of my life.

Everyone at Bella Books has been a pleasure to work with and I really appreciate the marvelous job Judith Fellows did on the cover.

I would also like to thank my editor, Katherine V. Forrest, for being there when I was first finding my identity as a lesbian. I cannot overstate the influence her characters and stories had on me. The five-page letter she included with her edits taught me an incredible amount about writing and connecting with readers. Without her thorough editing this work would not be complete. Of course, any errors that remain are my own, alone.

Dedication

Dedicated to those who gave me shelter and support and kept me sane while I worked on the recovery of my home. While there are many more I owe thanks to than I can name here, the generosity of John, Fran, Jennie, Ellie, Gavin and Linda will never be forgotten.

About The Author

After a decade of running bookstores for Borders and Music, Mary Griggs turned her attention toward nonprofit management. In 2001, she started Pacific Training and Resources, a consulting firm which offers organizational development consulting to not for profit organizations. Additionally, she serves as Deputy Director of Political Affairs for Forum For Equality, a human rights organization that promotes good government and protects the rights of lesbian, gay, bisexual, and transgender people in the state of Louisiana.

This is her first novel.

http://www.marygriggs.com

CHAPTER ONE

Janet was so used to sleeping through screams and slamming doors that the question barely penetrated her consciousness. A light touch on her thigh startled her out of sleep and she bolted upright, her heart pounding as the seat belt tightened against her body. She blinked and realized that she was in a car with a man whose name she did not even know. Instinctively, one hand clenched her small pack and the other reached for the door handle.

"Where do you want out?"

She turned to the driver in confusion. "What?"

"Hello? We're in Pennington. This is where you wanted out, remember?"

"Right." Janet looked around. While she had been sleeping, they had covered almost a hundred and fifty miles.

"How about here?" the driver asked, as he slowed the big car down.

"Here" was a small park, surrounded on three sides by the red brick courthouse, city hall and library. Water splashed from a fountain in the center of the park where a monument stood. Janet knew just where each of her dead ancestor's names was inscribed on its length.

"It's perfect. Thank you," Janet said. "I appreciate you giving me a lift."

"Don't mention it." The taciturn driver kept his eyes on his rearview mirror in preparation for pulling back out onto the street.

"Thanks anyway." Closing the door behind her, Janet stood on the curb, basking in the heat as she watched the sedan drive away. The air conditioner had been turned up high and she was relieved to finally be warm again.

As she blinked in the hot Alabama sun, Janet's gaze fell on a modest building across the street. The restaurant might have a fresh coat of paint and new sign but she remembered when it had been called Mama's Place.

With a glance each way, Janet crossed the street toward the restaurant. She glared up at the bells that jangled noisily as she pulled open the door. After years of alarms sounding for every entry and exit, she loathed having her presence announced.

The waitress looked up from filling salt shakers. Smiling broadly, the full-figured blonde called out, "Welcome to Sallie Lee's." Wearing a tight-fitting T-shirt emblazoned with *Sallie Lee's—Simple Food, Well Done* in red letters, she waved a blue, four-pound box of iodized salt nonchalantly at the marbled Formica lunch counter. "Have a seat here for faster service."

Janet gazed around the empty restaurant. The place was decorated in early diner chrome with maroon vinyl and tile accents. The tabletops were a bright white and the walls were decorated with paintings and photographs from local artists.

Raising an eyebrow at the idea that service to the sole customer would be a factor wherever she sat, Janet let the door swing closed behind her. "Quite a crowd you've got here," she said, sarcastically. "You sure you can seat me without a reservation?"

"We have the supper to-go crowd going to be coming in any minute, so you won't be alone for long," the waitress replied tartly.

"All right," Janet answered mildly.

She moved over to the long counter, dropped her backpack to the floor and sat down. Janet picked up a laminated menu card from beside the chrome napkin holder. The metal shone so brightly she could see herself in it. She had just started to read the menu when the waitress moved in front of her.

"You want something to drink to start off? We've got coffee, soda, iced tea and lemonade."

The waitress looked to be in her late twenties. Her blond hair was pulled back into a ponytail and when she smiled, Janet could see her crooked front tooth. The small imperfection was disarming and Janet felt a bit of guilt for her earlier attitude.

Before Janet could make a drink decision, another woman came out of the back. "I've finally gotten the dishwashing sanitizer running again. I'm really starting to think that that machine hates me." She appeared frazzled, her white chef's coat stained with yellow and red sauces. Her long dark hair was kept off her face in a single braid and she impatiently pushed a stray strand behind an ear.

Taking in the newcomer with a single glance, she smiled broadly. "Welcome to my place. Is Della tending to your every need?"

"She's trying."

"I don't see a drink in front of you."

"Oh, I'll have a lemonade, please, ma'am."

"Good choice," Sallie Lee complimented her. "That vintage is especially good today."

"Tell her you like it, she squeezed the lemons her own self," Della said out the side of her mouth as she moved by them both to fill the glass from a big pitcher.

Sallie Lee asked, "What can I get you?"

"Do you have any recommendations?"

"This is my place, sugar. I would be foolish to offer anything I wouldn't recommend." Sallie Lee crossed her arms. "Do you want to go for a sandwich or try a potpie?"

"I'm not much of meat pie fan. What kinds of sandwiches do you have?"

"I'd give the meatloaf a try. Moist with just a hint of heat."

"Okay. I'll have that and fries."

"Coming right up," Sallie Lee promised as she walked back into the kitchen, hips swaying suggestively as she moved. Janet's eyes lingered on the woman's backside before she sighed and dragged her attention back to the counter in front of her. This was neither the time nor the place to be cruising a total stranger, she admonished herself.

The hanging door to the kitchen swung shut behind Sallie Lee as the phone rang. Janet watched as Della picked it up and wrote up a quick order. Afterward, she walked to the kitchen door and gave it a shove.

"Lee, Luke Fox wants four hens in a bowl with a lid on wheels," she called out.

"Got it," came the strong voice from the kitchen.

When Della returned to wiping down the counter, Janet asked her. "What did that mean—hens in a bowl?"

"Chicken soup. With lids means the potpie and wheels on means that it's a to-go order."

"Kind of complicated."

"You have no idea." Della grinned and leaned closer. "Don't tell anyone that I told you the code," she whispered.

"Why? You'd have to change it then?"

"No, darling. I'd have to kill you." She snapped a wad gum between her teeth and walked back over to answer the ringing phone.

While Janet waited for her meal, the phone continued to ring. Most all of them were for Sallie Lee's fresh made chicken potpies. The waitress and the chef worked well together, preparing the orders, bagging them up and taking the money from the men and women who rushed in to pick up their dinners on their way home. Sallie Lee and Della joked with their customers as they made quick work of the rush.

Janet was kept entertained throughout her meal by the antics and banter. The sound of her straw slurping up the last of her drink surprised her and she looked mournfully down at her empty plate.

Sallie Lee sauntered over. "Can I get you a refill on your lemonade?"

"Thank you, yes," Janet answered, smacking her lips. "This is good stuff. I can't remember the last time I had a glass of real lemonade." Holding out the glass, she asked, "Tell me, is there a cheap hotel in town?"

Sallie Lee smiled. "No, dear. We don't even have an expensive one. It has been years since we've had enough visitors to sustain a hotel or motel. Everybody just passes through on their way somewhere else."

"Oh." Janet was shaken by the news. She had planned on finding a place to stay while she got her bearings.

Sallie Lee poured another glass of lemonade and put it down in front of Janet. "Isn't anyone expecting you?"

"No, ma'am."

"Kind of a strange place to stop then. This place is smack in the middle of nowhere."

"There used to be a couple of motels down on Route 128 but they closed after the interstate opened," Della added.

Janet bowed her head and sat silently. She felt almost lightheaded from the bad news. Clasping her hands together, she concentrated on breathing deeply until the feeling of panic subsided. A young psychiatric resident had once taught her about using deep breathing to promote relaxation and to manage strong emotions. She needed to practice it now more than ever.

"Have you ever been here before?" Sallie Lee asked suddenly, eyeing her more closely.

Janet looked up, her eyes briefly making contact before darting away. "Here? No, I've never been in your restaurant before," Janet equivocated automatically.

"It's just that you look real familiar." Sallie Lee replied with a smile.

Janet automatically smiled back and saw that it was triggering a memory. "I get that a lot," she answered as she schooled her expression. She stood and reached into her pants pocket for her wallet. "What do I owe you?"

Sallie Lee told her the total and Janet left a tip out of the change. With a nod to the owner and waitress, she shouldered her backpack and headed outside.

On the street, she froze briefly in panic. This day was turning into one of her nightmares. Not only did she not have anywhere to stay but she had not expected anyone to recognize her. Considering how good the meal was Janet regretfully decided that she needed to stay away from the restaurant in the future.

The heat of the day was starting to ease and there was a slight breeze that played with her hair. She took a deep breath and then another for good measure and could feel her shoulders loosening slightly. She pushed her bangs out of her eyes and looked both ways down the quiet street. As she crossed over toward the town hall, she wondered where she was going to spend the night.

Janet shivered. She had not expected to react so strongly to returning. Closing her eyes, she breathed in the muggy, late afternoon air and listened to the gentle splash of water in the fountain. Things sure sounded the same, she thought with some surprise.

She opened her eyes again and slowly turned around in a complete circle. The town looked exactly like she remembered it. There were no new buildings or any development at all in sight. Even the trees seemed to be the same size. She was almost disappointed that the town had not changed as much as she had. She had half expected to not be able to recognize anything.

Shaking her head at herself, she walked over to the memorial obelisk and read the names of those who had died protecting this small corner of Alabama from foreign foes. She paced around it and traced her finger over her uncle's name from the Vietnam War and her great-great-grandfather from the War Between the States. Most of the families in the town had at least one member's name up on the monument. Seeing how little space was left, she mused that if there was another war, there would not be any space left for their names. Given the deserted feel to the square, she guessed that there were not that many potential soldiers left in town.

Setting her backpack on the ground, Janet sat on the edge of the fountain. She wet her bandana in the water and ran the damp cloth over her face and the back of her neck. She felt stale and the dried sweat felt gritty under her fingers. Even though she had managed to clean up a little at the gas station restroom before bumming a ride, it had been three days since her last shower. With no motel in town, she wondered when she would next be clean.

For a moment, she questioned whether returning was a good idea. Slapping her palms on her thighs, she dismissed that line of thought as a waste of time. She was here and she would deal with whatever came her way. Janet climbed to her feet and slung her pack over her shoulder. With a determined step, she left the park and crossed the street.

She thought that she should start by walking over to her old high school. She remembered spending summer nights as a kid in the pecan grove behind the school stadium. The students would scare each other with the story of newly freed slaves being burned alive by vengeful whites in the grove following the Civil War. Supposedly, their ghostly wails of terror could be heard most summer evenings and it was a badge of honor to survive a night camped out in the grove.

If she remembered correctly, there was a firepit in a small clearing along the boundary between the back of the bleachers and the start of the grove. Janet hoped it was still there and that it would prove to be a safe place to spend the night.

She strode the four blocks to the school and was astounded at how small its concrete block walls were. Casually glancing around, she made sure that she was alone before she slung her backpack over the chain-link fence that ran around the school property. She then slid herself between the post and gate. The fit was a bit tighter than when she was a student but she managed to squeak through without losing too much skin or tearing her clothes. Janet grabbed her pack and moved as quickly as she could to the trail leading down to the track and football field. Once there, she was no longer visible from the street and she took the time to study her surroundings.

Kudzu had engulfed the slight hills on either side of the home bleachers and had even spread to cover the surrounding trees. The lush invader and its ability to grow a foot a day in the summer had defeated the best attempts by the school's staff to contain its spread. She could see the glint from soda cans and bottles that were nestled among its green leaves. The footing was treacherous and she moved carefully downhill, hoping not to scare any snakes into biting her.

Concerned that some maintenance people might still be around, she quickly checked behind and around her for signs of life. Janet froze when a squirrel moving into deeper cover shook a branch in front of her. She took a calming breath and continued to make her way across the track and football field to the visitor's bleachers.

The transition from the bright heat to the cool dark was refreshing. She made her way beneath the bleachers to the farthest corner from the school, scuffing through candy wrappers and cigarette butts. The area behind that section of the visitor seats was overgrown and Janet had to force her way through blackberry brambles. She had begun to worry that the area might be too wild to risk camping out in when she broke through to a small clearing.

Several logs were laid around a firepit. The ash in the circle of stones couldn't be more than a week old. She shook her head at the idea that those horror stories continued to be shared with the next generation of students. It amazed her that this place was still being used.

Janet walked around the clearing before choosing a spot away from the trees. She unrolled her sleeping pad and got a fleece blanket out of her backpack. She pushed her way farther into the woods before dropping her pants and squatting to pee. Once she returned to the campsite, she lay down and stared up through the greenery at the sky darkening from orange to purple to full dark. She fell asleep as the first stars appeared.

CHAPTER TWO

"Y'all take care," Della called as the last of the potpies was carried out the door. She turned the deadbolt and closed the blinds. "We're clear, Lee."

"Good job. I just have to finish this batter. What's left for you to do?"

"I've got that last customer's dishes here and I'll close out the register," Della said as she changed the radio station from country music to rock. "I should get hazard pay for having to listen to that crap all day."

Sallie Lee answered, "We've got an image to uphold as a country kitchen. The music twangs during business hours."

"Twang this," Della replied, as she made an obscene gesture and turned up the volume on No Doubt, singing "Hey, baby, hey."

"What did you say?"

"I didn't say nothing."

"Well, I heard something," Sallie Lee retorted.

"What you're hearing is a decent tune for a change." Della pulled out the ten-key and sat down with the drawer from the cash register. She laid out the bills in stacks and counted the change. Collecting the checks and credit card receipts, she began calculating the day's take.

Sallie Lee came out from the kitchen to grab the dish bin. "Good, we'll have a full load with these here."

Muttering to herself, Della slowly filled out the deposit form and put the cash and checks into the bank bag. She locked it and put the key in the cash drawer and the cash drawer into the small safe under the counter. "I'm done," she said, waving the bag at Sallie Lee. "You need any help back there?"

"Nope. The dishwasher is running and it's time to put this puppy to bed."

Della took off her apron and hung it up. She picked up her purse and went over to where Sallie Lee was waiting by the back door.

"Are you taking anything home to Daryl?" Sallie Lee asked as she took the bank bag Della handed to her. She reached behind the cabinet to turn off the lights and overhead fan.

Della laughed. "No, it's his turn to fix me dinner. He didn't go into the store today since he had that training up north all morning. The kids should be clean and the meal on the table when I walk in the door."

Raising an eyebrow in disbelief, Sallie Lee shook her head. "You've got the pizza parlor's number on speed dial just in case, don't you?"

"Yep," Della replied as she got in her silver Chevy Impala. "I'm more prepared than the Boy Scouts." She unrolled the window and called, "See you tomorrow morning. Do you need me to wait?"

"No, thanks. I'll just walk if she refuses to go anywhere."

Sallie Lee climbed into her Blazer and held her breath that the battery had enough juice to start the engine. Her younger sister had given her the SUV when, following the birth of her second child, she felt compelled to get a minivan. The truck had been growing more temperamental in the past year, making every attempt to go anywhere an adventure. She knew she needed to get a more reliable car but could not find the time when it was not working and did not have the energy when it was. The engine coughed to life, so she just sighed and put it in gear for the short drive to the bank where she made the night drop.

Sallie Lee nursed her car home and pulled into the driveway. She sat for a few moments looking at her house. It was her daddy's family home and the outside looked similar to what it had while she was growing up because she kept painting it the same bluish gray color and had never considering planting anything but the azaleas and camellias that had fragrantly surrounded the place since before her birth.

She got out of the Blazer and entered the house by the screened-in back porch. Putting one knee on the couch, she leaned over to reach the cord to draw apart the curtains and open the blinds of the living room before she crossed to the front door and collected the mail. The house stayed cooler with the blinds closed during the day but, at night, she liked sitting inside and watching the darkness approach.

Most of the furnishings were the same as when she inherited the house. Her older brother had already set up his home and did not need any of the furniture and her younger sister had an aversion to anything that reminded her of her past. Deep in thought about the history of her family home, she opened the rest of the curtains.

Sallie Lee walked upstairs to take off her shoes and change into shorts and a tank top. She had refurbished the master bedroom and bath on the second floor and had turned her old bedroom into a guest room. As she returned downstairs, she mused about what a great comfort it was to come into the same house in which three generations of Hybart women had cooked, cleaned and lived.

The kitchen was where the major modernization had taken place. She had installed state-of-the-art appliances and updated the lighting. She had also added a large workspace for preparing food and replaced the laminate countertops with granite.

Opening up the old-fashioned pantry and laundry room into the larger space of the kitchen gave the entire side of the house a feeling of space. She loved being able to come home from all day at the restaurant and still feel energized enough to be culinarily creative.

Tonight, she peeled a couple of eggplants before she sliced them thinly and sprinkled them with salt. All day she had had an urge for Eggplant Parmesan. Her version was almost eggplant pasta and it took only about a minute to cook. She carried the completed meal into the living room and ate it in front of *Headline News*. After watching the main stories from the day, she switched to The Weather Channel for the next day's forecast. She saw pretty much what she expected, more heat and humidity, and turned off the television to sit in the dark. Her mind went back to the stranger who had come into the diner.

Sallie Lee was bothered by the memory of her smile. She was sure that this woman was no simple traveler who had wandered randomly into this small town. Thinking best on her feet, she began pacing around the house as she worried at the stranger's familiarity. Frustrated, she plopped down at the piano in the parlor. After playing a couple of scales, she looked up at the family pictures on the cabinet. Standing up to get closer to the portraits, she was flooded with memories when she saw a picture of her younger sister in her high school cheerleading uniform standing next to a girl with a large camera.

That girl was smiling broadly and her eyes fairly shone with mischief. Except for having no wariness in her eyes, the girl in the pictures was unmistakably the woman from earlier today.

"My God," she murmured. She put the picture down and thought about how the two girls had been joined at the hip all through elementary and high school. Wherever the one girl was the other would not be far away.

Sallie Lee could not remember exactly what had happened to change everything all those years ago. She had been away at college that spring and had only heard bits and pieces when she came home for the summer. It may have been the biggest town scandal in fifty years but her parents would not tolerate any discussion of it in the house. She was not able to learn anything when she went out, either. Whenever she walked around downtown, all conversation would stop until she passed. Now, Sallie Lee was nagged by a sudden need to know the whole story.

Tapping her teeth with the nail of her index finger, she wondered how she could get more information at this hour. She remembered cleaning out the rest of her sister's things when she first started the renovations on the house and taking them up to the attic for storage. She was almost positive that the box of memorabilia from Julia Ann's school days was still up there gathering dust.

Sallie Lee went into the kitchen and pulled down the stairs to the attic. The attic was oppressively hot and she immediately began to sweat. She toyed with the idea about forgetting it all and going back downstairs into the air conditioning before she determined to at least see if she could find the box of her sister's stuff. If she were lucky, all of her sister's things would be together.

The two bare bulbs did not offer much in the way of light but they did attract several mosquitoes. Brushing them off her sweaty face, Sallie Lee made her way under the eaves to where she thought her sister's things might be, careful to step only on the plywood sheets lying over the exposed insulation.

She found the box and carried it back downstairs to the kitchen table. She quickly drained a glass of iced tea and washed her face and hands. The box was filled with newspaper articles, track ribbons, a varsity cheerleading letter sweater and hundreds of old photographs. The clippings were yellow and brittle and many had been torn carelessly out of the newspaper. Sallie Lee spent some time trying to figure out the chronological order.

The story that she finally pieced together had been written eighteen years ago on the scraps of paper laid out before her. An unidentified young woman had wandered naked and bleeding onto Route 17. A passing truck had nearly hit her before another motorist stopped and helped her get to the hospital. Her injuries were serious. A concussion, a ruptured spleen and she had been sexually assaulted. There were other, more minor injuries.

She flipped past clippings of editorials decrying the decay of society to the first mention of a missing teenager. She found a small piece, more concerned with the highlights of Jonathan Garrett's high school football career than the fact that the young man had not returned home after the homecoming dance. Sallie Lee read in the next article that his body was found the following night in the same area as the girl had been rescued. The police promised a complete investigation and the boy's family offered fifty thousand for information leading to the arrest and conviction of those responsible for his death.

Engrossed in her reading, she turned to the next paper and its scandalous lead story. The young woman, now identified as Janet Bouton, accused Jonathan of dragging her into the woods and assaulting her. She remembered trying to fight him off but had no memory of how she got away nor could she explain how he became injured. The article hinted at other misdeeds from Jonathan Garrett's past but did not elaborate.

She shuffled through the rest of clippings. She felt almost ill as she read that the Garrett family had accused Janet of making up lies. They denied that their son could have had anything to do with Janet's injuries and blamed her for the murder of their child. Her injuries, they claimed, were minor and self-inflicted. Other articles contradicted their claims and cited the motorist who picked her up and the hospital reports as proof that Jonathan might have killed her if she hadn't protected herself. Jonathan's bad end, it was speculated, only served him right.

Sallie Lee set aside several articles that had alternate theories of the crime. At least one reporter was convinced that someone else altogether had interrupted the boy's assault and killed him while allowing her to escape. He cited reports of the presence of an unidentified car parked by the woods that night and multiple footprints, many too large to be Janet's, around the body.

There was a gap of several weeks between that article and the next. The yellowing clipping described the beginning of the trial. Sallie Lee read that the district attorney was pursuing manslaughter charges against Janet. Again the various stories in front of her varied from those who defended Janet's right to defend herself against assault and those who believed she had lured him into the woods in retaliation for his stealing her girlfriend, who also happened to be her best friend.

Sallie Lee remembered that her sister had been devastated to be mentioned in the paper and subpoenaed at trial. The Hybart and Bouton families had been close and Julia Ann and Janet had been best friends almost since birth. The crime and publicity destroyed all of that. The prosecution had portrayed Julia Ann as the apex of a love triangle, whose deviant friend killed the man who stole her affection.

Examining the dates on the remaining clippings, Sallie Lee surmised that the trial had only taken a week. The prosecutor based their case on the fact that Janet and Jonathan had entered the woods together and only Janet had walked out alive. The article reported that the district attorney spoke of her unnatural attachment to her best friend and that her jealousy gave her a motive to want him dead. Further, it was reported that excerpts from a recording of her police statement were played to the jury and the court heard Janet describe in her own words being forced into the woods. Offering that as an additional reason for why she killed him, the district attorney closed his case against her.

The defense tried a couple of strategies. First, the lawyers put her doctor on the stand to witness that she was physically incapable of wielding the fatal blow because of her own injuries. Second, there was no evidence that she ever touched the rock that split his skull. Finally, they argued that anyone else could have killed him, including members of the opposing team that had stayed in town after the big game. Janet herself never took the stand.

The final clipping in the box was of the verdict and sentencing. Janet had been found guilty of manslaughter and was sentenced to spend two to fifteen years in the women's correctional facility in Tutwiler.

Sallie Lee remembered how withdrawn her sister had been throughout the summer following the trial. She would not go outside in daylight and refused to go anywhere in public at night except for her long walks around the neighborhood. Her despairing parents ended up sending her to Atlanta to live with their cousins for her final year of high school. Julia Ann had gone on to a university out of state as well and always found somewhere else to go for vacations. Since their mother's burial eight years ago, Julia Ann had not been back.

Shaken by what she had learned, Sallie Lee wondered if she was ever going see Janet again. She shuddered to think what else that poor woman had been through. Absorbed by her thoughts, she brewed herself a cup of tea and carried it upstairs.

Her reading chased even the idea of sleep away. She decided to take a bath before heading to bed, hoping the relaxing soak would ease her way to sleep. When she had worked on the house, she had redone the master bathroom to include a Jacuzzi tub and had never regretted it. No matter the heat of the day, after a long day in the kitchen she looked forward to the pulsing jets and hot water.

She pulled a well-worn mystery paperback off the shelf in the hallway. Dick Francis was a comfort when things seemed out of control or beyond comprehension. His predictable tales always had good winning over evil and the guy getting the girl. She ran hot water and poured just a dab of verbena-scented bubble bath into the tub. She undressed and scrutinized herself critically in the mirror. *Not too bad for forty*, she thought, as she turned sideways to view her profile. Her tummy had a paunch that wasn't there when she was twenty but, overall, she had kept her athletic figure. She raised her arm and vowed to shave her armpits tomorrow. Pulling the skin tight around her eyes, she laughed at the face a plastic surgeon would give her. *I'll keep them*, she thought of the wrinkles. *I earned them.*

Sallie Lee climbed into the large tub. She lowered herself slowly into the water, getting accustomed to the heat. Powerful jets quickly filled the tub with bubbles. They rose to eye level before she attempted to bat them down. Giving up on reading while the bubbles were so high, she just lay there, letting the watery fingers ease the tension from her back and legs and mind.

CHAPTER THREE

Sallie Lee woke up early the next morning with a pounding headache and an aching jaw. Last night's sleep had been filled with bad dreams. She stretched slowly then threw back the covers. After a quick straighten to the bed, she headed to the bathroom to take a much-needed cool shower.

She flipped on the radio as she brushed her teeth and listened to the weather report as she dressed. The perky female voice on the radio assured her of another day of over ninety-eight percent humidity. She pulled on a sundress and headed outside to cajole her truck into turning over.

A little over an hour later she parked in the alley behind the diner and entered the kitchen. The first thing she did was pull the waffle batter she had prepared last night out of the refrigerator to warm it up slightly. Then, she started mixing the ingredients for biscuits.

"Howdy, partner," Della called out as she came in an hour later. She started the coffee brewing before heading into the pantry for her apron. "Getting those kids off to school this morning was worse than pushing a string. I swear, they know when I'm running late and deliberately come up with ways to make me even later."

"I think you give them too much credit," Sallie Lee answered as she dusted flour off her hands and walked to the front door to unlock it. "You told me the other day they were angels for bringing you breakfast in bed." She opened the blinds and straightened the poster advertising the local community theatre production of *Annie Get Your Gun*.

Della pulled the cash drawer out of the floor safe and put it into the register. "Yeah, but I didn't mention the mess they made of the kitchen in doing it."

"You know you love it and them," Sallie Lee responded. "Hey, could you bring me some aspirin once the coffee is made?"

"Bad night?" Della asked solicitously. "You haven't taken up the vice of your brother, now have you?"

"I didn't have a drop to drink last night. I just had some nasty dreams."

Della glanced over her shoulder and waggled her eyebrows. "Ooh. Anyone I know?"

Before she could respond, the bell rang to signal the entrance of their first customer. Shaking her head at the saucy waitress, Sallie Lee headed back into the kitchen to await the first order.

"Waffles for four, one country pig and two crispy brothers," Della sang out as she put the slip on the rack. She slid a full coffee cup and the bottle of aspirin onto the counter. "This should start your motor running."

"Thanks, doll."

Things were fast and furious until nine o'clock when most everyone who was going to work was finally headed that way. The diner patrons who remained were mainly people waiting for the downtown shops to open.

Sallie Lee used the lull to start the preparation work for the lunch crowd. She began slicing tomatoes for sandwiches and setting out the few remaining chicken potpies from the freezer. Only a few lucky patrons who ordered early would get one of those. She was elbow deep in chopped potatoes for french fries when she heard the bell above the front door jingle.

"Well, you look like something that even the cat wouldn't bother to drag in," Sallie Lee heard Della say. She peeked out of the kitchen to see the woman from yesterday gingerly lower herself down on the same stool.

She was pallid under a layer of dirt and leaves. Her hair was sprinkled with twigs and a suspiciously shaped shadow discolored her jaw.

"Could I have some coffee before you abuse me too badly?" Janet asked.

Sallie Lee tried to reconcile the vibrant but wary person she had met yesterday with the pale woman sweating in the early morning cool. She looked physically beaten, Sallie Lee mused to herself.

Della laughed. "Sweetheart, when I begin to abuse you, you'll know it."

"Sorry. I'm just…uh…not feeling so great."

"Do you want something light then or something filling?"

"Filling." Janet shrugged and winced. "I'm hungry."

"Good, because if you liked supper, you're going to like breakfast."

"What've you got?"

"The typical fare but our specialty is waffles. How about I bring you some of the best ones you'll ever put in your mouth?"

Janet tiredly nodded. "That sounds great. Could I get some bacon with it? And a glass of orange juice?"

"If you're buying, I'm bringing." Della turned and slapped the slip onto the counter a few inches from Sallie Lee's curious face.

"Whoa."

Della looked curiously at her. "Were you eavesdropping?"

"What? Me? No! I was just waiting for the order," Sallie Lee answered, flustered.

"Whatever."

The restaurant was empty by the time Janet wiped up the last bit of syrup with the final bite of waffle. Sallie Lee had been watching her through the open door to the kitchen, trying to figure out a way to ask her why she had lied last night.

Janet pushed her plate away and saw Sallie Lee staring at her. Tipping her coffee cup at the cook, Janet said, "That was a fabulous meal. You ought to be listed in Zagat."

Sallie Lee came out of the kitchen with a basket of clean flatware and sorted it as she answered. "Thank you. That is especially kind coming from the daughter of such a good cook."

The cup in Janet's hand froze in midair for a brief moment before it continued its trip to her lips. She sipped before answering. "I don't know what you mean."

"I spent a good portion of last night trying to place you. I finally remembered about this young girl who got into trouble and left town."

"If she were trouble, that might be for the best." Janet pushed aside her plate. "Now, how about you give me my bill and I'll get out of your hair."

"You're Janet Bouton, aren't you?" Sallie Lee stated accusingly, staring at her. Della looked confusedly between the two women but stayed quiet.

Janet lost the small amount of color she had gained by eating and held up both hands in surrender. "Please, I don't want to be a bother. I'll get out of here as soon as I pay you."

"You're not bothering me." Sallie Lee leaned toward her. "You were best friends with my sister, Julia Ann. We used to call you two the J-Birds."

"I haven't spoken to her since before...um, before the trial." Janet swallowed noisily. "How is she?" she asked hoarsely.

"Married with two kids. She lives outside of Atlanta." Sallie Lee shook her head. "She left here the same summer you did and only comes back for funerals."

"We never said goodbye." Janet looked up at her. "You're her older sister, Lee, right?"

"Yeah, I went by Lee in high school. But, when you open a southern diner, you must have a down-home name." She grimaced. "I used to hate my parents for saddling me with Sallie Lee. I never fully realized the commercial applications."

Della interjected, "At least your parents didn't name all their children after states. My parents had the clever idea of naming us after the state we were conceived in."

"You're kidding, right?"

"Nope," Della replied. "Della is short for Delaware. I have sisters Virginia and Georgia and one brother, Tennessee."

"Incredible. Were your parents traveling sales people?"

"Dad was in the air force and Mom followed him from base to base."

Janet asked, "Do you still resent them?"

"Not really. Most of us got over that a while ago. We all have dinner at their house once a month in Montgomery. I think the fear that we may put them in a home in retaliation for our names adds spice to the relationship." She and Sallie Lee laughed together.

Janet smiled with them and held out a ten-dollar bill. "It was good seeing you again. I have to go now."

"Where are you going to go?" Sallie Lee questioned her. "I don't know what happened to you last night or where you stayed."

"I found a place to crash."

"Well, you got away with it last night but the sheriff doesn't take too kindly to people loitering in his town."

"He's not the only one," Janet answered, sourly. "I got the message loud and clear from his goons and I'll be heading out of town now."

"How? There's no bus service out of Pennington."

"I can walk."

Sallie Lee looked critically at her. "To be honest, you don't look like you could get very far without falling down."

"I'll be fine. I can take care of myself."

"I'm sure you are good at doing that. You just look like you could use a little help."

Della interrupted their conversation. "Honey, you need to sit down before you fall down."

Janet regarded her without speaking, although she did stop

swaying. Sallie Lee glanced at Della before continuing. "Why don't you come to my house? You can get cleaned up and recover from whatever happened to you."

"No, I couldn't impose."

Sallie Lee put her arms akimbo and leaned toward her. "And why not? I seem to recall that you spent many a night at our place growing up."

"Things have changed," Janet replied. "You don't even know me."

"I don't think things could have changed that much. I know who you were and I'm willing to bet that you are still the girl I remember."

Janet took a deep breath and winced in pain. "I can't even remember that girl." She looked at the two women on the other side of the counter from her. "I don't even know why I came back."

"Maybe home called you back," Della answered. "Maybe you came back to remember."

Snorting in disbelief, Janet responded, "So far it's been a pretty painful walk down memory lane."

"So let us help. Della, you can mind the store for a while, right?"

Della answered more for Janet's benefit than Sallie Lee's, "Things are very slow until lunch. Anyone who comes in now will just want coffee. Go on, girl, let her take you home."

"I don't know what to say."

"Then just say thank you and get your stuff together."

"Are you sure about this?"

Sallie Lee handed Janet her backpack. "Yes. I'm sure this is the right thing to do."

"Thank you," Janet said softly as she took the pack from her and followed her through the kitchen and out the back door.

CHAPTER FOUR

The air conditioner had barely managed to make a dent in the oven-like temperature of the car before they were turning in front of a two-story house. Janet glanced down at her watch and looked at Sallie Lee with her eyebrow raised.

Sallie Lee shrugged and said, "I know I'm close enough to walk to work but it's too darn hot."

"I didn't say anything," Janet replied. She looked at the house sitting nestled between a large oak and several magnolias. It was the same color that she remembered.

Sallie Lee pulled the car into the gravel driveway and got out. Janet followed her slowly. She stopped for a moment to observe the neatly trimmed lawn and shrubs before she gingerly climbed onto the back porch.

"Is it all coming back?"

"Yes. I'd know this place anywhere."

"I've only made a few cosmetic changes in the downstairs." Sallie Lee looked at the pale woman as she unlocked the back door. "How about I give you the two-cent tour—show you the bathroom and a bed?"

"That sounds nice."

"If I remember correctly you spent enough time here as a kid. My mom was pleased to have another daughter without the morning sickness and hours of labor."

"Your mom was always nice to me. I used to think of her sometimes..." Janet paused for a long time before continuing, "in prison." She glanced at Sallie Lee. "It doesn't get any easier to say that to people."

"Makes no matter to me. Mom would have liked to know that she was remembered fondly. I know she worried about you. Come on upstairs." Sallie Lee took the stairs two at a time and called over her shoulder, "I turned Julia Ann's room into an office. My old room is now the guest room."

Janet was only partially up the stairs. She had to use the handrail to pull herself along. She glanced up to see Sallie Lee staring down at her.

"Are you okay?"

"I'm fine, thanks," Janet answered too quickly. The pallor on her cheeks also gave lie to her words but Sallie Lee just nodded and continued talking.

"All right. Let me put some fresh towels in the bathroom."

Sallie Lee opened the linen closet and pulled out a washcloth and a Turkish towel. She glanced at Janet standing on the landing panting slightly from the climb. "Are you sure you're all right?" At Janet's nod, she asked, "Do you remember the fights between me and Julia Ann over who did what in the bathroom?"

"Yeah. You two really got into it," Janet said between gasps.

"I almost think we hated each other then."

"Do you get along now?"

"We've mellowed with age and not having to share a bathroom anymore." She ushered Janet into the guest room. "Anyway, the sheets on the bed are clean. Take a shower, have a nap. I'll be back around seven tonight."

"Thanks," Janet said.

A moment later, Sallie Lee came back through the door. "Hey, why don't you give me your clothes? I can toss them into the washer on my way..." Her voice trailed off.

Janet had taken off her shirt and it was dangling from her fingers. There were fresh bruises all along her side.

"Gracious, honey," Sallie Lee gasped. "What happened to you?"

"It's okay," Janet insisted as she turned away and raised her shirt up to hold it defensively in front of her chest.

"That looks like a boot print."

"It is."

"Who did this?"

"Some maintenance guys from the school."

"You spent the night in the grove, didn't you?"

"Yeah. It was just like I remembered it. Well, except for the whole getting my ass kicked part."

"They could have killed you."

"Tell me about it."

Sallie Lee reached out and almost touched the bruising on the right side. She halted when she saw Janet flinch. "That looks really bad. Can I take you to the hospital? You may have cracked something."

"Really, it's not that bad."

"Look, a friend of mine is a doctor and I'm sure she'd be happy to examine you."

"No. Thank you. I'll be fine," Janet repeated with emphasis.

"I'm sure you will eventually but I'm talking now."

"Could you just drop it, okay?"

"Why won't you go get help?"

Janet turned away from her and stared out the second story window. "I can't pay," she whispered, clutching the shirt in her hands. "I don't have any insurance and I don't have enough money to afford a trip to the doctor's."

"I can pay the doctor and you can pay me back."

"I don't want to owe you or anybody anything."

"Owing somebody doesn't mean they own you."

Janet clenched the shirt in her fist. "I don't want to be in debt," she growled stubbornly.

"Look, you used to work in your mama's place. I mean, you know how to cook and clean, right?"

Janet reluctantly nodded.

"Fine. You can work off whatever the doctor visit costs by doing that at my place. I warn you, though, I'll work you hard."

Janet turned and looked back at Sallie Lee. There were tears in her eyes.

"Does that plan seem fair?" Sallie Lee asked her.

"Yeah, but…" Janet started to argue.

"No buts. We're going tomorrow morning." Sallie Lee nodded decisively and held out her hand. "So, give me the rest of your clothes and I'll throw them in the washer on my way out."

Janet stood still, appraising her for a long moment before she handed her shirt to Sallie Lee. "This is really awfully generous of you."

"Nonsense."

"No, I mean it. Why are you doing this?"

"I think anybody would do the same."

Janet shook her head. "You're wrong there. You're a rare breed."

"Rare or not, I'm doing what I think is right." Sallie Lee took the clothes as Janet peeled them off her body. "Do you have any more dirty clothes?" she asked. "This is hardly a load."

Janet opened her backpack and pulled out a couple of T-shirts, socks and underwear. "I'm sorry, that's all I have."

"No. This is good." Sallie Lee seemed to suddenly realize that her sister's best friend was standing before her in the nude. She backed out the door. "I'll be back for dinner," she threw over her shoulder as she nearly ran downstairs.

Janet stood in the bedroom, staring at the door until she heard the car pull out of the driveway. She shook her head, trying to understand how things could change so much in such a short time.

Last night, she had slept well, as the clearing was quiet. The maintenance people, who obviously had orders to check out that particular clearing regularly, woke her up. Their way of getting her up was to kick her several times.

They pummeled her exposed back and sides with their booted feet. One of the men shouted that they did not want homeless trash ruining their town. They finally left with threats to finish her off if she was still there when they returned.

As fast as possible, she had gathered the rest of her stuff together and headed away from the clearing. When she got to Main Street, she remembered how welcoming the women had been at the diner the night before and decided to take a chance that she had not been recognized. She never figured that she would get more than a meal. She did not understand how she had gotten invited into Sallie Lee's home.

It was not just the home. She was standing in what was Sallie Lee's old bedroom. The wallpaper was different but the furniture was the same and arranged identically. She remembered sneaking in here when Julia Ann's sister was out. With a trembling hand, she stroked the bedcover to check if it was real or if she was dreaming.

Janet walked cautiously into the large bathroom and spent a moment just appreciating the size of the space. Finally, she reached into the stall and turned on the shower. Stepping inside, she shivered with the pleasure of finally getting clean. She spent a long time under the hot spray before she reached for the shampoo. The pleasure of massaging the lather into her skull was tempered by the ache caused by holding her arms up. She hummed a little while rinsing out her hair.

She held the glycerin bar to her nose, breathing in the floral scent. Finally, she soaped away the last of the dirt and grime. Janet turned the faucet to add more hot water to the spray. She enjoyed not being rushed out by a guard or by barely warm water running out.

The towels were another luxury. She had spent years with government issue and then low-rent hotel towels that were rough on the skin and could not soak up much water. The thick plush was every bit as good as she remembered.

Sallie Lee had put out a new toothbrush for her and Janet gratefully cleaned her teeth. The sharp minty taste brought back memories of when she and Julia Ann would have sleepovers. The two of them would laugh so much that they would spray the mirror with toothpaste, giving Julia Ann's older sister another thing to yell at them about.

She put on the robe that hung behind the bathroom door and made her slow way downstairs to find the washing machine and put her clothes in the dryer. The machine was still on the final spin and so she looked around the kitchen while she waited.

Scattered on the table were old newspaper clippings. She only had to see one headline to know that all the clippings were about her case. She read the top article about the sentencing and was lost in memories when the timer on the washer went off and startled her. Her sudden move nearly brought tears to her eyes and she had to hold onto the table until the sharp pain in her side dulled down again.

Feeling desperately tired, Janet put the wet clothes into the dryer and climbed back upstairs to bed. The sheets were cool against her skin and she was slowly able to relax her tense muscles. Between one thought and the next, she fell into a deep sleep.

CHAPTER FIVE

At the first real lull after lunch, Sallie Lee called her doctor friend. "Ida, I have a couple of questions for you. How concerned should someone be about possible broken ribs?" She twisted a strand of hair around her finger. "Well, there are a lot of bruises on the back and side." Sallie Lee straightened up. "Danger of what?" she exclaimed. "Broken ends puncturing a lung? Internal bleeding?" She felt vaguely ill. "What are the signs?" she asked. "Oh, you need an X-ray to know for sure." She drummed her fingers on the counter. "I've got a friend I want you to look at." She laughed. "Just a friend." Nodding, Sallie Lee said, "All right. As soon as I can."

As she hung up, Della asked her, "What was that all about?"

"That woman I took home has some bad bruises on her back

and sides. I think that's why she looked like death warmed over today."

"She didn't look hurt when she was in here last night."

"No, she didn't." Sallie Lee pulled a spray bottle of degreaser out from under the sink and began to clean the kitchen floor. "I wonder what happened to her?" she mused.

"Did you ask her?"

"Yeah, she got roughed up but no details."   Sallie Lee shook her head. "I have the feeling she wouldn't have answered me if I pushed it." Putting her questions aside, she focused on mopping.

Tired and anxious, Sallie Lee was glad to leave work at seven o'clock. Entering the house, she immediately checked the laundry. She had been afraid for the past couple of hours that Janet might have sneaked away before she came home. Seeing the open lid of the washer, she panicked until she opened the dryer door. If Janet had left, she had left all her clothes as well.

Sallie Lee removed the three shirts, one pair of pants and socks and three pairs of underwear from the dryer. She slowly folded them. She rested a hand on the meager stack before carrying them upstairs.

Pushing open the guestroom door, Sallie Lee saw that Janet was still asleep. The young woman was naked and the sheet was only covering her legs. Sallie Lee gazed at her for a long moment, her eyes lingering on the small breasts. Janet's torso was much paler than her arms.

Sallie Lee entered the room and placed the folded clothes on the dresser. She turned to leave but was tempted to take another peek at the sleeping woman. Her eyes roamed up Janet's body to her face. She flushed when she caught Janet looking back at her.

"Sorry. I didn't mean to wake you. I was really trying to be quiet. I just brought your things up. They are right there. See? Over there on the dresser," Sallie Lee babbled.

Janet pulled the sheet up to her chin. "Thank you."

"I'm going to start dinner now. Come down when you're ready." Backing out of the room, Sallie Lee caught sight of a slight, knowing smirk on Janet's face. That was too much to take and she fled all the way outside with her cheeks burning.

She went to the back garden and picked several tomatoes. The plants were a little bedraggled as the summer heat had wilted most of the greenery. Sighing, she regretted that she never seemed to have enough time to spend out in the garden. As she turned to head back inside, she saw Janet, clad in clean khaki shorts and T-shirt, watching her from the porch.

"Would you like me to water out here?" she asked.

"Thanks, that would be great," Sallie Lee answered gratefully. "I'm amazed everything isn't already dead from neglect." She looked around the garden. "I always have good intentions to come out here regularly and take care of the plants properly."

"Path to hell and all that," Janet responded. "Things come up and we get busy. Don't beat yourself up about a couple of thirsty plants."

"Gracious, you make me feel so much better."

"No problem." She walked into the yard. "So, where do you keep your hose?"

"On the side of the house, over there."

"You want me to hit the plants around the house as well?"

"Thanks. I'll be in the kitchen."

They each went their separate ways to handle their chosen chores. Sallie Lee skinned and sliced the tomatoes before she turned her attention to the cheese. "Son of a..." she cursed as she shook her bleeding knuckle. It never failed that she ended up including body parts when she grated cheese.

Stirring the mayonnaise, herbs and cheese together to form the filling for her pie, she hummed tunelessly. She took the tomato slices and lined them along the bottom of the pie shell she had already pulled out of the freezer. Once the filling was poured over it all, Sallie Lee slid the pie into the oven and set the table. She was flipping through the day's mail when Janet quietly entered the kitchen and pulled out a chair. She sat heavily down at the table.

"Why did you lie about never being here?" Sallie Lee asked suddenly.

Janet visibly started. "I didn't actually. I have never been in your diner before." When Sallie Lee said nothing, just stared at her in disbelief, she continued, "I didn't want there to be a scene.

I don't know if anyone remembered or even cared but I didn't want to take any chances."

"Fair enough." Sallie Lee gathered up the newspapers from the table. "From what I read, things were pretty bad. I can't believe you came back."

"I don't have anywhere else to go," Janet answered softly.

Sallie Lee placed a warm hand on her shoulder. "I'm glad you came here."

"Thanks."

"I'm going to change clothes and then dinner will be ready," Sallie Lee told her. "Could you start a kettle of water for tea? The pitcher is in the cabinet by the fridge and the tea is in a jar in the pantry."

"Sure." Janet got up to do the small chores.

Sallie Lee came back down wearing shorts and a tank top. She saw Janet sitting at the table with her head resting on her arms. Shaking a pill bottle, she said, "I've brought you some painkillers. You can take them after we eat."

"Good. I'm a little sore."

"I can tell that's an understatement just by looking at you," Sallie Lee retorted.

At the sound of the timer, she turned to the oven and pulled out dinner. The fragrant smell of cheese and herbs filled the kitchen. "We need to let this sit and rest for a few minutes." She spent the time washing the preparation dishes.

After ten minutes, she set a piece of savory pie in front of her guest. "Tell me honestly. Should we go to the hospital now or can you wait until the morning?"

Janet leaned on one elbow as she cut into her meal. "I can wait."

"Are you just saying that because you don't want to go at all?"

"I don't like hospitals," she mumbled around a mouthful of savory pie.

Sallie Lee laughed. "Neither does anyone else. Nobody in their right mind likes hospitals." She chased a large piece of tomato around her plate. "Should have cut these into smaller bits."

"This tastes good."

"I appreciate you saying so. It's quick and easy and that's what matters after a day over a hot stove." Sallie Lee folded her napkin and looked across the table at her guest. "What are you hiding from?"

Janet's head jerked up. "What are you talking about? I'm not hiding from anything."

"Of course not. You just snuck back into town because you didn't want anybody to throw you a parade."

"Okay, so I was a little careful and I lied to you. I'm afraid of how people will react when they know who I am."

"You were just a kid."

"Who killed a real stand-up guy and her own parents from grief for good measure."

"So, you remembered what happened? The papers wrote that you didn't know what happened after he dragged you into the woods."

Huffing out an annoyed sigh, Janet said, "No, I'm just saying what everyone has been thinking."

"Get over yourself. It's been almost twenty years. Most everyone who knew all about what happened are long gone. Nearly the entire high school left town for college and has never come back. Those that do know wouldn't care," Sallie Lee stated.

"Can you be sure of that? This town has vivid memories of the War of Northern Aggression and there's nobody still alive who fought for Dixie."

"I can be sure that it matters less than you think," Sallie Lee said. "The Garretts did themselves no favors when they pressed for your conviction."

Janet rolled her eyes. "Right. They suffered so."

"I can't speak for them. I can only speak to the fact that no one even remembers what happened or holds you responsible."

"Too bad none of you were available to testify at my parole hearings."

Sallie Lee pushed her plate aside. "I am so sorry about what happened to you."

"I don't need your pity."

"Look, brat, I wasn't offering any. I just want to help you. No strings."

Janet shrugged her shoulders in apology. "I'm sorry I bit your head off. I'm not used to being treated like this."

"I'm sorry that treating you like a human being is so unusual. Maybe you should have come back sooner."

"I'm not even sure why I am here now." Janet pushed away her plate. "I really appreciate you taking me in. You're very kind."

"You're welcome. If you are done there, why don't you head back to bed?"

"I can help with the washing up," Janet offered.

"Not tonight. You need to rest. I will be getting you up pretty early tomorrow morning."

"All right. I'll give in tonight but I won't be so easy tomorrow."

"Easy, yeah. That's exactly the word I would use to describe you."

A fleeting smile crossed Janet's lips. "On that note, I'll say goodnight."

CHAPTER SIX

Sallie Lee groaned when the clock radio clicked on at four o'clock. At such an early hour she did not care what the news highlights were so she cut Carl Kasell off in mid-sentence.

She dressed quickly and went into the other room to wake up Janet. She watched her for a moment; Janet was lying on her back and her breathing was rapid and shallow. "Rise and shine, kiddo," she said brightly. "Time to see the doctor."

At the first word out of Sallie Lee's mouth, Janet's eyes snapped open. For a moment she just lay still before she tried to move. Then with a mumbled curse, she pulled the sheet off and seemingly attempted to talk herself into the effort it was going to take to sit up.

When Sallie Lee leaned over her, she said, "I'm up."

Sallie Lee simply stood beside the bed with her arms crossed.

"What?" Janet asked. "Can't you see that I'm ready to go?"

"Do you need help?" asked Sallie Lee.

"I don't know yet," Janet responded tiredly.

Visibly holding her breath, Janet struggled to sit and then stand up. She took a couple of steps closer to her clothes and used her proximity to the dresser as a convenient prop. Her pants were lying just out of reach on the chair.

Sallie Lee shook her head and handed the pants to her. She silently watched her struggle into them.

"Wait," she said when Janet tried to put on a T-shirt. She left the room and returned with a shirt that buttoned. The bruising was much more extensive than she had thought yesterday and was a riot of colors on Janet's back and side. Sallie Lee wondered how smart it had been not to insist that Janet go immediately to the emergency room.

"Ready to try the stairs?" she asked once Janet had slid her feet into her shoes.

"You didn't install an elevator last night by any chance?" Janet asked wistfully as she gazed down the staircase.

"I wish." Sallie Lee walked backward down the stairs, staying within arm's reach of Janet as she laboriously descended.

With gentle hands, she eased Janet into the truck and then had the usual early morning fight to get it to start. Eventually, she ended up using a spray start right into the carburetor to get it to run.

When she got back into the truck she was cursing, "Mother-loving mess of trash."

Janet chuckled softly. "Please, don't make me laugh. It hurts too much."

"I swear I will get a new car and turn this thing into a birdhouse," Sallie said seriously. "Mark my words," she threatened, "you will rue the day you took me on." She knocked her knuckles on the dashboard.

"Rue," Janet repeated, before she laughed again. "Stop it, you're killing me."

Sallie Lee laughed with her. She glanced quickly over at Janet after driving over an unevenly patched bridge. She saw her bite her lip and stifle a cry.

Driving slowly to the Urgent Care Clinic, Sallie Lee divided her attention between her passenger and the road. Janet was hunched over in the seat and hugged her elbows to her sides.

"Hold on, honey," she implored her. "We're almost there."

Sallie Lee parked out front and let Janet lean on her as they made their way into the waiting room. Janet took no notice of the paperwork the nurse tried to hand her. Sallie Lee accepted the clipboard and asked the nurse to check if Dr. Forest was available.

Dr. Forest was winding up her overnight shift and she came out of the back when the triage nurse announced their arrival. She was a large, dark black woman and she opened up her arms upon seeing Sallie Lee and the two women hugged.

"Girl, you're a sight for sore eyes."

"Ida, how can you work all night and still look so good? There ought to be a law."

"Actually, there is a law but the good ole boys are too scared to enforce it," she laughed. "So, what have you brought me this time?"

"My friend, Janet, that I told you about. She might have some cracked ribs."

Janet stood in front of them staring at the floor and shifting from side to side.

"Hello, Janet," Dr. Forest said gently, holding out her hand. She smiled when Janet reached out and quickly squeezed and released her hand. "Why don't you come on back with me?" she asked as she headed through the door to the examining area.

Janet did not immediately follow. She just looked at Sallie Lee pleadingly.

"Can I come too?" Sallie Lee asked her friend.

"Sure thing," Ida answered. "If Janet doesn't mind, then neither do I."

"Please," Janet said desperately.

Sallie Lee squeezed her arm gently. "Don't worry. I'm coming with you."

They went into a small examining room. Beside the table were two chairs and a small desk. One wall had a light box and the other a built-in cabinet. "Is there anything in your medical history I should know before we get started?" the doctor asked her.

"No, ma'am," Janet whispered.

"All righty then. How about you take off your shirt?" Dr. Forest asked her.

Janet winced slightly as she worked it off her shoulders. Her entire right side from armpit to hipbone was mottled with bruising. There were clear boot print marks on her back. Sallie Lee held a hand to her mouth. Ida shook her head warningly as Sallie Lee started to speak.

The doctor reached out to touch Janet's back and the young woman flinched. "I'm going to touch you now. Are you ready?" She waited for a nod before she continued. "This is going to hurt," she cautioned as she pressed her hands along Janet's spine. She slowly moved her hands over the young woman's back and side. "Just hang in there, kiddo. I'm almost through."

When she was done, Janet was pale and panting. Dr. Forest made a couple of notes before handing her a thermometer. "Put this in your mouth."

While they waited for a reading, the doctor took hold of her wrist and felt for a pulse. At the end of a minute, she winked at Janet. "One-forty-five. Maybe I should have taken your pulse first." When Janet didn't respond, Dr. Forest glanced at Sallie Lee. The monitor on the thermometer beeped.

"At least you don't have much of a fever." Dr. Forest put the stethoscope in her ears. "Take a deep breath," she asked as she listened to Janet's lungs. "Again."

When Janet coughed after one deep breath, Ida picked up the receiver and called for a nurse. "I will need a set of chest films, Henrietta. Could you go with her to the lab and do her vitals again while you're there?"

"Of course, Doctor," the gray-haired nurse answered. Wearing scrubs covered with pink and blue teddy bears, she tenderly helped Janet into a hospital gown. "Please, follow me," she said. Leaning together, the two of them made their slow way out.

"What happened to her?" Dr. Forest asked Sallie Lee as they watched them walk down the hall.

Sallie Lee shook her head. "A maintenance crew chased her out of the grove. She came into the diner yesterday morning and was like this."

"I really wish you hadn't waited."

Sallie Lee held up her hands. "I was lucky to get her here at all."

"Do you know what she's afraid of?"

"She spent some time in prison. I guess that kind of experience could make it hard for anyone to handle being kept somewhere against their will."

"You could be right. Although, I would put her aversion to being touched down to sexual trauma." Dr. Forest wiggled the blank chart. "I get the feeling she isn't going to fill any of this out."

"I don't think so either, Ida. Is that going to be a problem? There won't be an insurance claim. I'm putting this on my plastic," Sallie Lee explained.

"Can I trust you two not to sue me?"

Sallie Lee smiled at her. "And lose my best friend and best source of gossip?"

"If I do this, you'll owe me the entire story," Ida warned her.

"If you do this, I'll owe you more than that." Sallie Lee grinned at her, "How about my firstborn?"

Ida shook her head. "Thanks but no thanks. I am having enough trouble with my own spawn." Eyeballing Sallie Lee, she asked, "Anything else I should know about what happened? Is she injured anywhere else?"

"Not that I could see." At Ida's raised eyebrow, she blushed and confessed, "I saw her without much of anything on yesterday."

"Hmm, you'll have to tell me all about that later." Ida peered down the hallway to see that Janet was walking back toward them. "Well, I need to know so I can treat her. Will she answer me or is she more likely to tell you?"

"I don't know. I knew her as a kid and I think she trusts me but you're the doctor." Sallie Lee shrugged. "Why don't you try it?"

The nurse handed Dr. Forest the still damp film. She put it on the light box and pointed out a couple of greenstick fractures.

"Janet, did whoever beat you also sexually assault you?" Doctor Forest asked without turning around.

"No," she answered firmly. "Just the ribs."

"Are you sure? I could examine you, if you want."

"They just kicked me, okay?" Janet replied. "Nothing else happened. I should know, right?"

"Good. Let me tape you up and you can go back to Sallie Lee's home to rest."

Janet glowered at Sallie Lee. "I'm going in to work with you."

The doctor said sharply, "Don't try to be a hero. You need to rest so that the bones can knit back together. Give it at least another day before doing any real bending, lifting or turning."

Ida picked up a roll of under wrap. She had the nurse help hold Janet's arms up and away from her body. With quick, economical moves she wrapped and then taped Janet's chest. "That should help some but I'm going to prescribe some pain medication as well. Are you allergic to anything?"

Janet shook her head as the nurse eased her back into her shirt.

The doctor led the way back to reception where Sallie Lee pulled out a credit card to pay for the visit. Ida handed her the prescription and a couple of individually wrapped pills. "If she seems to have any problem breathing, bring her back. Call me if she develops a fever. I put the prescription in your name, so you can get it filled."

Sallie Lee smiled gratefully at her friend and gave her a hug. "Thanks. I'll have you and Butch over for dinner soon."

"You better. You owe me the story."

Waving airily, Sallie Lee collected Janet from the waiting area and assisted her back into the truck. "I'm going to drop this prescription off on my way to work and bring it to you after the lunchtime rush."

The drive home seemed to go by quickly. Sallie Lee helped her into the house and put her on the couch downstairs with the TV remote in reach and an afghan over her lap.

"Here, take this," she told Janet, holding out one of the pills

Ida had given her. She watched carefully as Janet swallowed. "I'm going to leave a bottle of water here, in case you get thirsty," she continued as she placed the bottle on the coffee table. "Try and get some sleep."

She watched Janet's eyes close and gently brushed the hair off her forehead. When the dark eyes opened again, she smiled. "I'll be back around three. Take another pill at noon."

Janet nodded and closed her eyes again. She was asleep and lightly snoring before Sallie Lee's truck cleared the driveway.

Sallie Lee opened the back door of the diner only a half hour later than usual. She marveled that all her running around this morning had not taken more time.

She was stirring and muttering to a big vat of grits when Della walked into the kitchen.

"Lord, woman, you look like one of Macbeth's witches," Della told her. "Could you be any scarier?"

"What are you talking about?"

Della waved a hand in her direction. "The steam, the bubbling cauldron, the incantations, the dark circles under your eyes."

"I didn't sleep very well last night."

"How is your house guest?" Della asked as she put on her apron.

"Took her over to the Urgent Care this morning. She has a couple of cracked ribs."

"Where is she now?"

Sallie Lee added the butter before she answered. "On my downstairs couch."

"Are you sure about this?" Della inquired. "I can understand you taking her in yesterday but shouldn't she be moving on now?"

"Do you know her story?"

"No. I even asked Daryl if he recognized the name. After a bit of hemming and hawing, he recalled that there was a Bouton a couple of grades ahead of him in school but he couldn't recall the specifics last night. He seemed all weird when I tried to get him to talk about it."

Sallie Lee covered the pot and put a rack of bacon in the

oven. Over the next half hour, she recounted the story to Della in pieces as she came in between customers and to pick up orders.

"How brutal," Della said when she finally finished. "I can't believe she had to spend all that time in jail for killing the creep that raped her."

"No kidding. They'd never be able to get a conviction today."

"Shoot, no one would dare press charges. The whole thing is bogus." Della bit her lip. "But are you really responsible for her?"

"Our families used to be close. She and my sister were inseparable before all this happened. I think I owe it to her to help."

"And how is your sister going to feel about you having an affair with her?"

Sallie Lee nearly dropped the chicken she was holding as she turned on Della. "What do you mean by that," she demanded.

"I know you are a generous person but, even for a saint, you opened up your house and your heart pretty damn quick. It doesn't take a genius to see that she has gotten under your skin."

"What? I—"

Della held her hands up against whatever Sallie Lee was trying to say. "Your voice gets softer when you talk about her and your eyes light up when you're thinking about her. I just want you to be careful."

Sallie Lee knew she was visibly upset and did not care. "You are way over the line."

"Maybe I am. But I love you and don't want to see you hurt."

Whatever Sallie Lee was going to say was interrupted by a bell ringing by the register. "You've got customers waiting," she said pointedly.

"Lee," she started to say but Sallie Lee turned her back on her. Della bit off the rest of her sentence and headed out to the front.

Except for the necessary conversation to get the food onto the tables, there was none of the usual interaction between the two women. It was late morning before Della came back into the kitchen. "Lee, I have a fellow out there who wants to know how you get your grits so creamy."

Sallie Lee was struggling with the dishwasher sanitizer. The flow kept jamming on her and she was trying to trace the cause by following the hose. "Tell him with cream," she said impatiently from her position under the sink.

"Maybe you should tell him?" Della stated calmly.

Sighing dramatically, Sallie Lee crawled back out and made a great show of getting to her feet and dusting off her clothes.

Della shook her head at her friend and preceded her into the dining room. "Our chef will answer all your questions," she said grandly to the table of visiting fishermen.

"Ma'am, I haven't had such creamy grits in all my life. What do you do?"

Sallie Lee leaned in close. "It takes about an hour and both milk and cream to get them like this."

"An hour?" he repeated. "It only takes fifteen minutes at home."

"And see what it gets you. My way is slow and, let me assure you boys, slower is always better." She winked at the men.

"Amen, sister," affirmed an older African American woman at the next table.

The men laughed and tossed down money for their check and a generous tip. Sallie Lee sauntered back to the kitchen, feeling a little better.

The lunch crowd was thinning when Della came into the kitchen. "Lee, I want to apologize for what I said earlier."

"Can we not talk about this now?"

"Yeah. Okay. But we do need to talk before too long."

"I know." Sallie Lee sighed. "I know you have my best interests at heart. I am just not ready to hear it."

"As long as we're cool. Go on and take that prescription home. I can handle things until you get back."

CHAPTER SEVEN

Sallie Lee walked into the Rexall Drug store and waved at her young next-door neighbor in the magazine section. "Hey, Tommy."

"How do, Miss Hybart?"

"Fair to middling," she replied, heading toward the pharmacy counter in the back. "Shouldn't you be in school?"

"No, ma'am. I'm too sick." He sniffed dramatically.

"I see." Sallie Lee smiled. "I hope you feel better soon."

"Thank you."

"Mr. Foley, do you have something for me?"

The tall, bearded man peered over his glasses at her. "Why yes, Miss Lee, I do." He pulled a small, white bag out of the plastic bin. "You need to make sure you don't drive or operate heavy machinery while you're taking this," he warned her.

"I'll be careful."

"You also shouldn't drink alcohol with it."

Sallie Lee sighed. "Not a drop."

"Good, good. Is there anything else you need?"

"Actually, there is. Could you make me a chocolate malt to take away?"

The older man smiled kindly. "Of course. It would be my pleasure." He stepped down from the pharmacy counter and over to the small soda fountain.

Sallie Lee sat on the stool and watched him fill the beaker with ice cream and add the chocolate sauce and malt mixture. His movements were deft as he made her shake, just as they were when handling drugs. He placed the beaker under the old-fashioned stirring machine and then, moments later, poured everything into a tall paper cup.

"Do you remember Margaret Bouton?" she asked him.

Mr. Foley was clearly startled by the question. "Margaret," he repeated wonderingly. "I haven't thought about her in ages." He stroked his beard. "Lovely lady. Such a tragedy to befall her family."

"Do you know what happened to the kids?"

"It's been a while." He drummed his fingers on the plastic straw container. "I believe that Michael is making a career out of the army. And as for the girl, Janet, I haven't heard a thing since they took her away." Pulling out a straw, he asked, "Wouldn't your sister have a better idea about that?"

Sallie Lee shook her head negatively. "She lost touch with her."

"I shouldn't wonder. The whole thing was a mess. I was sure sorry to see what it did to Margaret and Stephan, though. Losing the restaurant was just another cruel blow. Sometimes you think that going like they did was almost a blessing." He wiped the counter and muttered, "Parenting is fraught with perils, and one never knows how the children will turn out." He sighed. "Why do you ask?"

"Someone came into the diner and remembered how it used to be."

"Well, you've got nothing to worry about on that count.

Mama Bouton would be right at home in the place you've made. Don't let anyone tell you otherwise." He rubbed his stomach. "Just thinking about your fried chicken livers and onions makes me hungry."

"I'll be sure and fix some for you next week."

"You are a sweet girl." He carried her bag and drink over to an antique cash register and punched the keys. "You didn't have your insurance card with the prescription. Did you want to give it to me now?"

"Oh, no. Don't worry about the co-pay, I'm not claiming these."

"If you're sure about that. It takes your total to $57.86."

"No problem." Sallie Lee handed him her credit card. "It's just easier this way."

"Whatever you say, young lady. I only work here." Mr. Foley smiled to take the offense out of his words. He slid the slip across for her to sign. "You take it easy. I wouldn't want you to end up in an early grave like your daddy."

"My heart is fine," she replied automatically, picking up her purchases and walking out.

She fumbled for a moment outside of the drugstore, blinded by the midday sun. She thought back to what Della had said and wondered about the condition of her heart as she got into her truck for the drive home.

Worrying about the time, she parked on the street instead of in the drive and let herself in by the front door. Janet was struggling to sit up but relaxed when she saw who it was.

"Sorry, it was easier to come in that way," Sallie Lee apologized. "I brought you a chocolate malt."

"Hey, thanks." Janet took a deep drag of the thick liquid. "Good stuff."

"Our local neighborhood drugstore has a genuine soda fountain right inside."

Janet wrinkled her brow. "The Rexall is still in operation?"

"Sure is. Old man Foley is still there, older than ever."

"That's incredible." Janet leaned back. "It's strange. I keep expecting major changes around here. But, everything seems to be just like I left it."

"You must admit we aged well."

Janet's expressive mouth curved into a smile. She glanced at Sallie Lee. "Some parts certainly have."

Against her will, Sallie Lee blushed. "Smooth talker," she retorted. "I have to get back. Take a pill if you need it."

When she opened the front door to the diner, Sallie Lee stepped into chaos. The place was so crowded she had to squeeze her way inside. Della was surrounded on all sides by senior citizens, all clamoring for her attention. Every seat in the place was filled and the noise was overwhelming. Upon seeing Sallie Lee, she gave a welcome cry of relief.

"Hang on, everybody. The cook is back and we will have your orders up in a flash." Della pushed through the crowd to the kitchen. "I am so glad you're back."

"What on earth happened here?"

"Seems their trip to the outlet mall has been interrupted by a blown gasket. The senior center's bus is over at Ray's Garage." Della grabbed another pitcher of lemonade from the fridge. "They descended upon us about ten minutes ago."

Sallie Lee washed her hands. "Give me a rundown of what I'm facing."

"Eight want chicken fried steak and gravy. I need fifteen potpies and four roast beef sandwiches. I turned on the stove, so it should be preheated by now." Della looked out into the dining room. "I'm going back out. Tell my kids I loved them."

"Shoo," Sallie Lee said fondly. "Food will be coming up and soon they will be eating out of your hand."

"Until then, they are just as happy to bite off my arm."

Sallie Lee laughed and tied her apron. She took the potpies out of the large refrigerator and slid them into the oven. She pulled out the roast beef and poured the container of gravy into a large pot to warm up. She was whistling to herself as she pounded the steak.

"A whistling woman and a crowing hen; neither will come to a good end."

Sallie Lee looked up and saw her old Sunday school teacher. "Mrs. Conner! It's been forever!"

"Hello, Lee," the vibrant elderly woman replied. "It's so wonderful to see you. I had no idea you were a restaurateur."

"I opened this place up a little over five years ago."

"I always thought you were going to be a big city reporter."

Sallie Lee quickly coated the steak in breadcrumbs, egg wash and then in the breadcrumbs again. "No, I came back after school and haven't left for long since."

"I was so sorry to hear about your mother."

"Thank you."

"How are your brother and sister?"

"Robbie is in Florida teaching at Gainesville. He and his wife have a kid in college. Julia Ann is married with two kids in Atlanta."

"Gracious, you all have moved far."

She sidestepped out of the way of Della coming through for more iced tea. "I need seven more chicken fried steaks," Della called as she headed back out to dining room.

"All with mashed potatoes and gravy?"

"You got it."

Sallie Lee saluted her with her tongs. "Coming right up."

"Do you have a particular fellow in your life?" Mrs. Conner asked once they were alone again.

"No, ma'am. I've, uh, been very busy with my business."

"Well, don't take too long with work that you miss out on love."

"No, ma'am." Sallie Lee turned the breaded steaks in the hot oil. "Ma'am, could I ask you a question?"

"Of course, child. What is it?"

"What would you say if I told you that I didn't think a man could bring me love?"

"What, dear?"

"I mean, what if I told you that if I fell in love with someone that person would be a woman?" Sallie Lee risked a quick glance at the older woman before she dished up some mashed potatoes to go with the plates of chicken fried steak.

"What are you saying?"

Sallie Lee debated dropping the entire issue but decided to push on. "I'm a lesbian, Mrs. Conner."

Mrs. Conner studied her for a long moment. "Child, I have always believed that God cares more about the fact that we do love one another than the actuality of who we end up loving. When I was a girl, there were plenty of people who would say that blacks and whites who intermarried were sinning against nature and they had laws on the books to see that it didn't happen." She smiled. "But it happened anyway because you can't choose who you love and the law finally caught up with common sense."

Walking into the hot kitchen, she reached up and held Sallie Lee's face between her hands. After studying her for a moment, she continued speaking, "In three of the Gospels, Jesus tells us that the greatest commandment is to honor God and the second greatest is to love your neighbor. If you do both of those, what person dare say you cannot enter the kingdom of heaven?"

Her eyes tearing, Sallie Lee said, "Thank you."

"Don't thank me, dear. Thank that nice young man from Galilee who made such an impact on this world."

"Yes, ma'am. I will."

"You better." The older woman shook a finger at her. "I haven't seen you at service in a long while. It's about time you came back to worship with us."

Shaking her head, ruefully, Sallie Lee agreed. "All right. I will do my best."

"That is all I have ever asked my students to do." She looked at the plates that were ready to go to the waiting customers. "Could you throw another steak on for me? They look mighty tasty."

"For you, I would do anything," Sallie Lee replied. "Have a seat and I will get it to you in a flash."

CHAPTER EIGHT

It was just after six the next morning when Sallie Lee opened the back door to the diner and switched on the lights. "In the room over there should be some clean aprons," she told Janet. "Start by putting one on." She glanced up from the refrigerator when Janet took up a position beside her, tying the apron strings.

"Good. We need to get a few things ready for breakfast. I'll have you start by shredding some potatoes for hash browns. Once customers finish their meals, I'll have you busing the tables."

"Okay," Janet answered softly. Moving slowly, she filled her apron with potatoes to wash. She carried the clean vegetables over to the worktable mandolin to reduce them to a fine shred.

Della came in and smiled at the two of them. "Good morning, sunshine," she sang out and twirled around in her long denim skirt. "Today is going to be a beautiful day."

"How do you figure that?" Sallie Lee asked as she turned on the oven and griddle.

"Because it started out so well. Daryl was very frisky this morning and I am all limbered up." She made a show of her newfound flexibility, rotating her shoulders and arms.

"Way too much information." Sallie Lee wagged a finger at her. "I don't want to know about your sick, little married perversions."

Della sniffed loudly. "Jealousy. Pure jealousy." She flounced out into the dining area to open the safe and turn on the register. "Are we ready?" she called, poised to unlock the door.

"Yeah, let the games begin," Sallie Lee answered.

In the lull before the first customer, Della tidied up the front counter and wrote the day's special on the board.

All three women worked well together. Janet was quiet but Sallie Lee and Della ribbed one another and the customers throughout the morning. As the crowds slowed down, Sallie Lee had Janet start the preparation for the lunchtime special.

"It's a two-day process. I roast the chicken and make the stock one day. The next day I make the pot pies." Sallie Lee dusted the work surface with flour and began to roll out the pastry. "My secret is to use a bit of the chicken fat that is rendered in the pastry in place of butter."

Della heard her. "Uh-huh. Makes the crust all meaty tasting. Once you have one of Lee's, you will never go back to Mrs. Swanson."

She put Janet to work chopping carrots, celery and potatoes. "I need everything in a small dice." She reached out and poked at a pile of carrots. "Maybe a little smaller than that. Perfect. Put them in bowls when you are done."

Della came in with her order pad. "Hey, Judge Jordan called. His jury is going to eat in so he will need potpies for the lot of them. Twelve plus two and he, the clerk and the reporter want one too. Make that seventeen altogether."

"Keep chopping, Janet," Sallie Lee said, "we've got pies to make and no time to waste!"

"How many pies do you make in a day?"

"Close to two hundred for lunch and another fifty or so for

take home at dinner. When I first opened I would close after lunch. I kept seeing how many people stopped off for pizza on their way home and wanted to capitalize on it without having to keep the dining room open after five o'clock."

Della strolled back in with additional take-away orders. "On Monday, Wednesday and Friday we have the potpies and Tuesday and Thursday we offer whatever was on the lunch menu."

Sallie Lee added, "Your mom had a good thing here. This is such a great location, with the courthouse and city hall right across the way. I'm not sure I would do so well if I was relying on tourist traffic."

Janet wiped her face with her sleeve. It was hot back in the kitchen but the delicious smells of the roast chicken and browning pastry made the proximity to the stove worthwhile. "Overall you seem a lot busier than I remember Mama's being."

"I think her numbers still beat me on weekends. No one is really around much anymore and the Sunday after-church crowd seems to shrink every year." Sallie Lee started to fill small casseroles with the filling. "I have a captive audience here in the downtown. Mike's Pizza and Ralphie's Barbeque are a little too casual for most of the folks at the courthouse."

"And this way they get their vegetables too," Della added. "Something their mamas can be proud of."

"That's true. We mustn't forget the nutritional benefits to home cooking."

"Or even the environmental. This place has a real good feel to it," Janet added. "And an even better aroma."

"Why, thank you, honey. That's possibly the best compliment I've ever received." Sallie Lee slid ten casseroles into the oven and began to prepare more. She peered through the steam from the boiling pots at the young woman. "You are starting to drag a little, Janet. Why don't you finish clearing up in here and then go out to the counter and have lunch."

"I'll be all right."

"I didn't say you would be otherwise. You should just take it slow."

Janet nodded. "Okay. I'll stop for lunch but only because I'm starving."

"Fair enough. I need more mushrooms sliced. Can you work on that for a bit?"

"Sure."

"The ones I washed earlier are gone. Take that basket, run them under the water quickly and use the brush to clean off the dirt."

Janet followed her instructions and brought everything back to the cutting board. "How do you want me to do these?"

"Quarter the small ones and slice the larger ones into about the same size."

The two of them worked quietly for a while. Della came in during a lull and emptied out the dishwasher and loaded it up for another run. When the timer went off, Sallie Lee told Janet to go and sit down.

She brought out a potpie to the counter. "I don't think I can eat all of this by myself," Janet warned.

"I wouldn't be too sure about that. They seem to disappear before your eyes," Sallie Lee responded. "Don't worry if you can't. I'll have a bite or two to finish off anything left over."

"Wow," Janet exclaimed after her first bite. "It tastes even better than it smells."

"It's nice to know that all your hard work went into something good," Della replied. She looked at the young woman for a long moment. "So, tell me what the boss was like as a kid?"

Janet took a fleeting glance into the kitchen. "I don't think the friends of younger sisters ever see the older siblings in the best light. She thought the two of us were annoying and we did everything we could to live up to her expectations."

"How about in school?"

"She was in her senior year when we started high school, so she didn't know us and we weren't to ever indicate that we knew her. She was involved in everything, though. Student council, float committee, captain of the basketball team; she was one of the untouchables."

"I can just see her as Queen Bee," Della smirked. "It's nice to know some things never change." She wiped down a couple of tables. "Was she stuck up?"

Janet turned to her. "I don't want you to get the wrong idea. Our families were friends, so we did hang out together."

"But not like buddies."

"No, the best times we had were when our families would go to the club together. We'd start out with a morning of golfing together. Our parents would be one foursome and Julia Ann, Lee, Robbie and me would form another." Janet smiled at the memory. "We would finish playing golf and then play doubles together, while our parents drank at the bar. I ended up paired with her against the other two. She could be vicious if I missed anything she thought she could have gotten to. I became a much better tennis player trying to stay on her good side."

Della laughed. "Yeah, she can still get pretty mean if you fail her."

Janet stacked her dishes and picked a rag up off the counter to wipe the area where she had eaten. "How did you end up here?" she asked.

"My dad was in the air force and when he retired, they settled near here. It's only an hour drive to Maxwell Air Force Base and the commissary." Della brought out a case of napkins and began to fill the table holders. "I came home from college and got a summer job at Harco's. Daryl was a manager trainee. Let me tell you, he was fine. Tall and handsome." She got a dreamy expression on her face. "I just kept coming back on vacations for more. We got married after I graduated."

"And working here? How did that happen?"

Della shook her head. "I couldn't find a part-time job after I had Randy, my second son. Nobody wanted to hire a mother with two kids under four. I was sitting in here bitching about it when Sallie Lee comes over and offers me a job." She looked fondly into the kitchen. "After the end of my first year, she let me buy into the place. I'm a part owner now." Della winked. "She's still clearly the boss, though."

Della worked quietly for a while. Seemingly making a decision, she came closer to Janet. "Can I speak frankly with you?"

"Sure. What's up?"

"Lee is my best friend."

"Uh-huh," Janet murmured noncommittally. She waited and watched Della.

"I'm serious about that."

"I didn't think you weren't." Her voice was mild.

"You need to be careful around her."

"She seems pretty strong."

"I am warning you to treat her nice."

"Well, thanks but I don't think I need warning."

"Don't take this the wrong way but she's a pretty important part of my life."

Janet held her eyes. "I don't doubt that."

"She's been alone for a while. I wouldn't want to see her taken advantage of."

"You mean by an ex-con," Janet answered bitterly.

"By anyone who wasn't planning to treat her with respect." Della sized her up. "I'm not saying you wouldn't be good for her in the long run. I just don't want her hurt."

"She's been good to me. I don't intend to hurt her."

"How long are you going to be around?"

"Does it matter?"

"It might if she gets too attached to you."

"Well, don't worry about me. I won't be here long enough for it to make a difference."

Sallie Lee took a step out of the kitchen. "Why the long faces?" She scrutinized the two women. "What are you talking about?"

Janet said, "I didn't know that Della was an Auburn fan. We were debating the merits of their short yardage passing plays."

At Della's belated knowing nod, Sallie Lee turned her back on both of them and threw her hands in the air. "Fine, don't tell me. I didn't really want to know."

CHAPTER NINE

At two o'clock the next afternoon, Sallie Lee told her to take off for the rest of the day.

"Why? I'm doing okay."

"You've been working hard all day and there is no reason for you to kill yourself."

"I'm fine," Janet replied.

"Whatever. Take the time to smell the roses for all I care."

Janet was aching enough to not keep fighting. "All right. I'll go."

"Do you want me to drive you home?" Sallie Lee asked, distractedly. She was in the process of cutting kernels off corncobs.

Janet rolled her eyes. "No, thank you. I can easily walk from here."

"Fine. I've got some extra corn on the cob I will bring home, so please put a big pot on to boil around seven o'clock."

"Anything else?"

"Maybe make a salad of what's still alive in the garden. I can't think of anything else right now. I'll call if something occurs to me."

"Cool." Janet waved goodbye to Della before heading out the door.

She started to walk in the direction of Sallie Lee's house but, before she went a block, her steps slowed and then stopped. She stood for a moment, thinking. She was not in the mood to spend the day inside. Maybe she actually should go find some roses to smell.

Janet turned away from the town center and walked toward the river. As a child, she made the trip regularly from her mama's restaurant to home. Like the Hybart's, her parents' home was within easy walking distance of downtown, albeit to the east of the town center.

As she got farther from Route 128, Janet could see the housing developments that Della had told her about. A lot of the houses were new and much closer together than she remembered the houses in the old neighborhood to be. Many of them seemed almost too big for their lot, leaving few of the pathways that she and Julia Ann used to use as shortcuts between each other's homes. Deep in her musing about the considerable changes to her old haunts, she almost walked by the lot where her house used to be.

She stopped and stared at the weed-choked empty space. Even the trees that shaded the backyard were gone. A dog barked at her from the front yard of the house next door but the street was otherwise quiet and still. Standing with the sun beating down on her head, Janet was struck by the sum of what she had lost. There was nothing to hold her here, on this street or in this town.

Very cold, all of a sudden, despite the heat of the day, she turned from the lot and strode further east toward the cemetery. With the house where she grew up gone, she needed to see the place where her parents were buried. She felt untethered and hoped that touching their stones would ground her again.

She came across a small bakery and a flower shop in the block before the graveyard. She smiled fondly at a memory from childhood. Once a month, her parents would bring her and her older brother out with them to tend their parents' plots. Her dad would cut the weeds and her mom would scrub off the stones. As youngsters, they collected trash and, as they grew more dexterous, painted the waist-high fence that surrounded the graves. As a reward for working hard, they would stop here for cookies on the way home.

The screen door banged shut behind her and she smiled at the young girl who stood up from behind the counter. The girl smiled shyly back in welcome.

"Do you still make Cinnadoodles?" she asked.

"Yes, ma'am. We've sold them for longer than I've been alive. How many do you want?"

"I'll take five, thanks."

As the girl collected and bagged her order, she asked, "Are you from around here?"

"I was, once."

The girl waved a hand up the road. "You got kin up there?"

Janet nodded and accepted the bag from her. "Yeah. Thanks."

"Sorry for your loss," the girl called out.

Her mouth full of the cinnamon sugar cookie, Janet just waved as she went out the door. She strolled up the wide tree-lined avenue that ended at the gates of the graveyard. The stately oaks and maples had stood sentry along the lane for almost two hundred years.

The cemetery was peaceful and still. Live oaks twisted around themselves, while ubiquitous kudzu encroached over the retaining wall. The only sound was the buzz of insects that hovered lazily in the cooler air under the trees.

Janet slowed as she neared her parents' final resting place. The wrought iron fence around the Bouton plot was rusting and was in need of a new coat of paint. The graves were covered waist-high with weeds and wildflowers. There were nine plots filling in the small area. A small bronze plaque marked the buried medal of her dad's brother. There had been no body to come back to them from Vietnam.

She put her bag of cookies down outside the gate. She had to force the rusted hinges to open and let her inside. The noise of the protesting metal silenced the crickets for only a moment. She stood alertly, listening to see if anyone would come to investigate, then continued into the area.

She placed her hand on the newest stone. Her parents were united in life, death and for eternity under this speckled granite. It was cool beneath her fingers despite the heat of the day.

Running her fingers over the date of their passing, she was filled with remorse. She brushed at the dirt on her fingertips and shivered, disturbed by the rundown condition of her family's gravesite.

Kneeling by the graves, Janet began slowly and then feverishly to pull up the grass and weeds that obscured the headstones. She was crying silently as she fought to clear the entire area. In her distraction, she quickly lost all sense of time or temperature.

It was almost nine o'clock when Sallie Lee came up to the gravesite. She had gone home directly after closing the diner and was concerned when Janet was not there. There was no note and no sign that Janet had even been in the house that day. She had waited for a while, pacing from room to room downstairs. As the hour grew later, she became seriously worried. Her instincts were telling her that Janet was in trouble. Sallie Lee debated going out and searching for her, tossing her car keys from hand to hand. Impulsively, she made up her mind to drive around to search for her. She made the decision to drive out to the cemetery after her cruise around the school yielded no sign of Janet.

It took her awhile to find the Bouton interment area in the gathering dusk. She had not been out there since their funeral thirteen years ago. The meandering paths and large oak trees hung with Spanish moss had never seemed so malevolent before.

The first thing she saw was piles of freshly pulled weeds all around the short wall enclosing the burial plots. As she got to the fence, she was very concerned to see Janet sitting on the ground in front of her parents' headstone, gripping her knees to her chest and rocking back and forth.

"Janet? Are you all right?"

Janet did not make any sign that she heard the gentle call. Sallie Lee stepped into the plot and squatted down next to her. She reached up and picked a stray leaf out of the dark hair.

"Honey?" she asked again as she placed a hand on Janet's tense forearm. She was concerned at how hot and dry the skin felt under her hand. Janet was not sweating.

Sallie Lee shook her gently. "Janet, please talk to me," she pleaded.

Janet turned her head and looked at Sallie Lee with no recognition in her eyes. Her face was dirty and streaked with tears. She blinked slowly and tried to focus on Sallie Lee's voice.

"What?"

"I need you to come with me, okay? Come on. Stand up." Sallie Lee talked softly to her as she tugged on her arm.

Janet's arms released their tight grip on her knees. Sallie Lee was dismayed when she caught sight of Janet's hands. They were swollen and there was blood on her fingertips where her nails had been ripped off. "What have you done to yourself?" she murmured.

"They couldn't see," Janet whispered.

"Who couldn't?" She put her hands under Janet's arms and attempted to hoist her upward.

"All this stuff was in the way," Janet said, resisting her as she held up a handful of weeds.

Sallie Lee took the stalks from her and tossed them to the side. "You did a good job. They can see clearly now." She squeezed Janet's shoulder. "We need to go."

Sallie Lee stood behind her and tried again to lift her from under her arms. Janet made an effort to shake her off. "Leave me alone," she mumbled.

"Janet, please help me. I can't do this by myself." After a couple of false starts, she got Janet to stand. Taking a deep breath, she struggled to get her turned around to face the exit.

"No!" Janet cried. "I can't leave them." Her eyes were wild and she took a stumbling step toward the headstone.

"You aren't leaving them," Sallie Lee assured her. "And anyway, they left you first." She smoothed Janet's hair and continued to talk softly. "Honey, they know how much you love them. They wouldn't want you to make yourself sick." Tugging gently on her arm, she was able to get Janet turned around and moving toward the exit.

"I miss them," she mourned.

"Of course you do." Pushing the gate with her hip, Sallie Lee forced it wide enough for both of them to pass through. "You had me worried when you weren't at home."

"I'm sorry." Janet started to cry as she stumbled on the broken sidewalk. She sobbed but there were no tears.

Sallie Lee grabbed hold of her arm and partially carried, partially dragged her back toward the truck. "I know you are, baby. Let's just get to the car."

They made slow progress to the Blazer and it was a struggle to get Janet into the passenger's seat and get her buckled in. The truck started on the first try, drawing a heartfelt *thank you* from Sallie Lee.

Janet had completely withdrawn again by the time they reached Sallie Lee's home. She spent the drive staring blankly at her hands. Sallie Lee tried to shift her out of the truck but Janet seemed oblivious. In desperation, she lightly slapped Janet's face until the dark eyes focused on her.

"Why are you hitting me?" she slurred, putting a hand to her pinking cheek.

"I need you to get out of the car," Sallie Lee answered.

"All right." Janet turned in the seat and slid off but once her feet touched the ground her knees buckled. Sallie Lee had to dive to keep her from collapsing. She braced the younger woman against the side of the truck.

"Stand up, damn it," she demanded angrily. "I can't carry you."

Janet mumbled, "Please don't be mad at me." With a great effort she locked her knees and stood without aid.

"I am not really mad at you," Sallie Lee explained as she

pulled Janet toward the porch. The two of them lurched into the house. "You're scaring me."

"How's that?"

Sallie Lee led her directly to the bathroom where she had Janet sit down on the toilet seat and hold onto the hand towel rack. She ran cool water into the bathtub. "I think you got way overheated and that is really dangerous."

"I'm dangerous?"

Putting her fingers under the running water to test the temperature, Sallie Lee answered, "Not you. Your temperature. We need to cool you down and rehydrate you."

She turned and looked at the young woman. "Okay, off with these clothes," she said, putting her hands on her hips.

"Why?" Janet questioned, plucking at her stained shirt and pants. "What's wrong with my clothes?"

"Because I'm not putting you in the tub with all your clothes on."

Janet giggled slightly at that. She tried to help undress herself but seemed surprised when she found it difficult to get her hands to work properly. "My fingers hurt," she told Sallie Lee, holding them out for inspection. In the harsh light of the bathroom the bloody and torn tips looked worse than ever.

"I know. We'll take care of them in a little bit." Gently she undressed her. "Okay, now you need to get into the water."

"Oh. It's cold," Janet complained after putting one foot into the water. She tried to lean away from the tub.

Sallie Lee pushed on her other leg. "Don't be such a baby. Get in."

After she got Janet into the water, Sallie Lee went upstairs and collected her first-aid kit. She came back and pulled a now shivering Janet out of the water. It was a struggle to get the slippery and rubber-legged young woman back to her perch on the toilet lid. Pulling out a pair of scissors, Sallie Lee cut the chest tape off and wrapped a towel around the trembling woman. She picked up a glass of water and held it to Janet's lips.

"Drink this," she said to her.

Janet took a long sip and leaned her head on Sallie Lee's shoulder. "My head hurts," she mumbled.

Sallie Lee held the glass up again. "You're dehydrated. Let's get more liquid into you."

After the glass was empty Sallie Lee made her get back into the water. When Janet started shivering again, Sallie Lee got her back out of the water and into the towel. She put a Thermo Scan thermometer in Janet's ear and was pleased to see her temperature was 100°.

"Have another drink," she ordered Janet.

Her hands were shaking and Sallie Lee had to help her hold the glass. "I'm so cold."

"Good. You were too hot before." She put down the empty glass. "Time for me to work on your hands," Sallie Lee told her. "Put your hands over the sink."

Janet complied and Sallie Lee took the opportunity to examine the damaged fingers. Two nails on her right hand and three on her left had torn off below the quick. There were blisters and slices on almost every finger. "Try and hold still," she warned as she poured half a bottle of hydrogen peroxide over Janet's hands.

"Ow," Janet exclaimed as she tried to pull away from the pain. "That really hurts."

"Shh," Sallie Lee said as she bent over and blew gently on her hands. "I'll make it all better."

"Make it better, my ass," Janet responded, no longer slurring her words.

Sallie Lee was relived to see that Janet's eyes were focusing. The worst of the heat stroke was fading. "Glad to have you back," she told her. "I need you to take one more plunge and then we can go upstairs."

"Do I have to?" Janet whined.

"Yeah, I don't want to take a chance that this is just a phase."

"You're just paying me back for not telling you what Della and I were talking about yesterday."

Twisting an imaginary mustache, Sallie Lee chortled. "Yes, I put all my victims in cold water instead of hot. Now, stop stalling and get in."

Sighing, Janet got back into the tub. She was sullen when

Sallie Lee handed her another glass of water. She had to finish it before Sallie Lee would let her out. By then she was shivering and she leaned into the dry towel that Sallie Lee wrapped around her. Janet needed Sallie Lee's help to make it upstairs.

Turning on only the nightstand light, Sallie Lee steered Janet to the bed. The younger woman was nearly out on her feet. Pulling up the thin cotton sheet, Sallie Lee watched Janet close her eyes and relax into a doze.

Sallie Lee left the guest room and returned with a bottle of aloe and a tube of triple antibiotic ointment. When she felt the bed sag with the weight of another, Janet's eyes opened and focused on Sallie Lee.

"Let me put this stuff on your face," Sallie Lee said, shaking the bottle. "And this on your hands," she continued, dropping the tube in her lap.

"Can't it wait? I'm really tired."

"You can sleep after I grease you up."

Sallie Lee worked for a few minutes before she was aware of Janet's eyes on her face.

"How did you find me? I didn't even know I was going to their graves."

Sallie Lee shrugged. "I don't know how I knew. It was the second place I went."

"Where was the first?"

"I drove by the school."

"That's where I went the first night I was back in town."

"I know. You always seemed to be fascinated by the grove. If I remember correctly, that was your camp out place of choice."

"Not just mine. Julia Ann liked going there too." She stirred slightly on the bed. "Thanks for coming to get me." She winced as Sallie Lee applied the ointment to her forehead. "I don't know what came over me out there. I think I went a little crazy."

"In this weather, that isn't too hard to do."

"I was lucky you came searching for me." Janet's eyes were closing and she struggled to reopen them. "Thank you."

Sallie Lee watched her fall asleep. "Anytime." Leaning down, she quickly placed a kiss on the other woman's nose. "Sleep now."

CHAPTER TEN

Janet came downstairs early the next morning to find Sallie Lee rinsing out her coffee mug. "It's late. Why didn't you wake me up?"

"Because you're taking the day off."

"Why?"

"I'm the boss and I say so." Sallie Lee pressed one damp finger into Janet's sunburned forehead. The skin whitened then quickly returned to a bright red. "You came pretty close to cooking yourself yesterday and you look it. Rest today and you can come back in tomorrow."

"I'd rather work than just sit around all day."

"In your current condition you'll scare my customers. I don't need lobster girl putting them off their feed."

"I'll stay in the back, really, I will."

"And do what? Look at your hands."

Janet obeyed. Her fingers were swollen and oozing. "That's kind of gross."

"And it's definitely a health hazard."

"I could wear gloves."

"Maybe tomorrow." Sallie Lee nudged Janet with her hip. "Hey, it will be all right. Just relax and enjoy the time off. You'll have the house to yourself."

Janet was scared at the idea. "It was being alone and thinking yesterday that got me into trouble."

"Maybe it wouldn't affect you so badly if you would just do it more often." Sallie Lee smiled at her. "*Nosce te ipsum.*"

"What does that mean?"

"It's Latin. It means know yourself."

Janet replied, "I remember a line from *The Outer Limits*. 'We so fear the unknown because we know ourselves too well.'"

Sallie Lee looked at her. "I'm afraid I can't agree with that one. I believe that knowledge is power and self-knowledge is the most powerful of all."

"Doesn't power corrupt?"

"Don't be silly. Power over others does. But you can't want to live in ignorance all your life."

"I thought ignorance was bliss."

Folding her arms, Sallie Lee asked, "Do you feel blissful?"

"Not particularly."

"Then why stay that way? What do you have to lose?"

Janet pulled on her earlobe. "I could lose the little I have left."

"You won't be able to keep what you do have without work. You've got issues, honey. The way I see it, you've got two choices," said Sallie Lee as she dramatically lifted her right fist.

Janet nodded at her raised hand. "Go on."

"Well, one, you can keep running. Leaving this town like you left all the others." Sallie Lee frowned. "I really hope you don't take that option. Two, you can stand up, figure out who you are, and maybe have a chance at happiness." Pointing her two fingers at Janet, Sallie Lee continued, "Don't try and tell me that you don't deserve it. I seem to recall a constitutional right to it."

"I believe that it's actually a right to pursue the elusive thing. The framers didn't have a thing to say about actually achieving it."

"I'm glad to know that the education this fine city bestowed on you didn't go to waste."

Janet smiled. "Mr. Porter left an impact on a lot of young minds. I don't know anyone else in my cellblock who could quote from the Federalist Papers." Her eyes lost focus as she stared into the past. "Can't say that I found the whole thinking thing of much use."

"Fine, if you don't want to think, read." Sallie Lee directed her into the living room and pointed at the many bookcases. "Plenty of choices in here." She went to a shelf and pulled out a paperback. "You might want to try this one."

Janet inspected the book. "*The Maze in the Heart of the Castle.* I never heard of it."

"It was my favorite book when I was a kid. You might like it. It's about a boy who has to try and figure out the maze within himself. It's a great adventure story and morality play. I've reread it again and again."

Reluctantly opening the proffered book, Janet answered, "I'll try it."

"Don't do me no favors, now."

Janet blushed. "All right, already. I'll read it."

"Good. I want you to take it easy until lunch. Drink plenty of water and use that tube of aloe if your face hurts. You can walk over to the diner around noon. Come have lunch with Della and me. Heck, depending on what you look like then, I might let you work in the afternoon."

"You'll let me?"

Sallie Lee affected a haughty demeanor. "I might or I might not. It depends on how your fingers are looking," she said.

They both looked down at Janet's hands.

"Don't risk my ire by overdoing it."

"I'll be there." Janet raised her mangled hands in surrender. "I'll take it easy now and plan on working later."

"See you later then." Sallie Lee headed out the back door to wrestle with her truck.

Janet turned the book over in her hands several times before she poured herself a tall glass of water and sought out a comfortable chair. In the living room, an oversized chaise lounge fit her perfectly. She turned on the table light and began to read.

She did not expect to be engrossed by a book for young adults but she was riveted by the story of an orphaned boy who learned to take his light with him. She was startled out of the story when the grandfather clock struck twelve times. With great reluctance, she marked her place and closed the book. Checking the time again, she cursed and took off for the diner at a fast walk.

Sallie Lee was insufferable after she wrung the information out of Janet that she did not want to put the book down to come into work. "Maybe now you will listen to me," she crowed.

"I didn't have to tell you anything."

"Of course you did. You feel better for having told me even though it means that I get to tease you."

Janet shrugged ruefully. "I haven't been teased in the longest time."

Walking up to the two of them, Della broke in, "Don't tell her that. She won't leave you alone now."

Almost too softly to be heard, Janet answered, "I hope not."

Sallie Lee blushed and bustled back into the kitchen. "It's pork chop day, so I'll need you to get to polishing the chrome. You'll find the rags and cream polish under the lunch counter."

"Be advised. You are going to find gravy in the weirdest places," Della added. "Here let me help you put gloves on."

Once her hands were properly covered, Janet picked up the polishing compound and tried to work. It was soon obvious that detail work was beyond her ability and she switched to just bringing items over for Della to polish.

Apart from requests from one or another to hand something over or to move out of the way, the women worked practically without speaking until five thirty. It was a comfortable silence that filled the restaurant and allowed them to quickly finish the cleanup.

"Good job, ladies," Sallie Lee declared. "You've helped make this place shine like the top of the Chrysler Building."

"We love you, Miss Hannigan," both women chorused in unison. They gaped at each other in amazement that they were channeling the orphans from *Annie* at the same time.

Sallie Lee looked at both of them with great fondness. "The pair of you are getting more insufferable every day."

"We live to serve." Della tugged on her bangs.

"Enough. Is everyone ready to go home?"

"More than ready," answered Della as she headed to her car.

Together, Sallie Lee and Janet locked up the restaurant and walked the short block to where the Blazer was parked.

"How about we head over to Belk's before going home?" Sallie Lee asked as they buckled up in the truck.

"Whatever you want to do is fine by me."

"Well, I'm thinking you need another set of clothes."

Janet peered down at her stained T-shirt. "I can't seem to stop spilling things on myself." She turned slightly in her seat to look at her driver. "But that doesn't mean that I need a new wardrobe. I haven't paid you back for the doctor yet. I don't have enough for a shopping spree."

"Spree? Who said anything about a spree?" Sallie Lee concentrated on the road, pulling onto the busy Route 128. "Look. I'm not talking about a wardrobe. Get another couple of T-shirts to wear at work. Also, you need a pair of jeans to replace the ones I spilled ammonia on yesterday."

"I can't keep taking from you all the time." Janet wiped her sweating palms on her legs. "I owe you more than I can repay."

Sallie Lee took her eyes off the road and glanced at her. "Janet, this isn't calculus where we have to keep track of who does what to whom." She gripped the wheel tightly. "I want to do things for you. I find myself thinking about what you need. What you would want if you would only let yourself."

Checking over her shoulder as she changed lanes, she put up a hand to stop Janet from speaking. "Let me finish this, okay?" She took a deep breath. "I don't want to own you or have you indebted to me. I want to help you because I want you to stay in my life. No strings."

Janet had to fight back tears. "I don't want you to care about me."

"Too late. It's done." Sallie Lee smiled at her. "Now, are you going to keep arguing?"

Rubbing the tears from her eyes, Janet nodded. "I should have remembered how you are."

"What do you mean?"

"Even as kids, it was always better not to cross you. Everything was just easier if we all did it your way."

Sallie Lee looked over at her in disbelief. "You make that sound like such a bad thing."

CHAPTER ELEVEN

It was early the next evening when Sallie Lee unlocked the back door to her house. "I have to hand it to you," she told Janet. "You put in one good day's work." She put the mail and her keys on the end table and headed to the kitchen.

"I'm going to try out this chicken dish on you," Sallie Lee called over her shoulder as she tossed several potatoes in a pot of water on the top of the stove. "I had a housemate from Puerto Rico and she claimed her family had been making this dish since Columbus docked."

She made quick work of chopping garlic and threw the rest of the marinade ingredients together. She placed several chicken breasts in a bag with the marinade paste and handed it to Janet. "Give this a good rubbing?" she asked.

Sallie Lee melted a stick of butter in the microwave. She

dumped partially cooked potatoes into a colander and sliced them, stopping often to blow on her burning fingers. Taking the bag back from Janet, she layered the potatoes and chicken in a casserole dish, poured the melted butter over everything, and slid it into the oven.

She sat down and wiped her face with the dishtowel. "Whew. I can't wait until this heat breaks."

Janet poured them both a glass of iced tea. "It's not the heat, it's the humidity."

"Yeah, that was one of the best things about living in San Francisco." Sallie Lee nodded at Janet's questioning look. "I spent a few years out there and prefer fog to humidity any day." She smiled at the memory of cold, damp summer days. "Sometimes I really miss it." She regarded Janet carefully before she asked, "Can I ask you some questions?"

"I guess. What do you want to know?"

"I never knew what happened for the diner to close."

Janet looked sadly at the tabletop. "They had to sell the business to pay my legal fees. Considering how badly I lost, you'd of thought the lawyer would be ashamed to charge as much as he did." She looked up at Sallie Lee. "I don't remember who the buyer was but they weren't able to keep it going without Mama in the kitchen."

"What happened to them? They passed a long while ago, didn't they?"

"They died soon after my first parole hearing. It was so hard on them to see me there," Janet sighed. "I had been accepted to Emory before everything happened. Everyone was so happy. Dad wanted me to be a doctor like him. Instead, he gets a daughter in prison." Janet slowly released her clenched fists. "I hated seeing what I had done to them."

"How did they go?" Sallie Lee probed gently.

"They went up to visit my brother over in Fort Bragg. He was graduating from Jump School." Janet cleared her throat. "On the way back, Dad fell asleep at the wheel and drove across the median and under an eighteen-wheeler." She glanced quickly up into Sallie Lee's concerned eyes. "I was told that it was quick; they never felt a thing." She scrubbed her fingers across her forehead. "They wouldn't let me out for the funeral. I can't get over that the last time I saw them, they were crying over my parole being denied."

Sallie Lee reached over and held onto her hands. "Where is your brother now?"

"I have no idea. I got one letter after Mom and Dad died telling me he was getting rid of everything. Nothing since."

"I'm so sorry."

"We weren't really close, even before things went wrong. He was starting high school when I was born, so we never really knew each other."

Sallie Lee squeezed her hands, stood up and got a spoon to baste the chicken. "Still, it had to have been hard on you," she said as she bent to peer into the oven.

Janet shrugged. "It's hard to miss what you never had."

"Don't be so tough about it. It had to have hurt."

Janet nodded. "Yeah. I felt kicked in the stomach after I got that letter. I knew I was alone before but it really hit me when even my brother wanted nothing more to do with me."

Closing the oven door, Sallie Lee returned to sit at the table. "You were sentenced to serve two to fifteen years. I don't think anyone believed that you would spend that long in jail." She paused for a second to find the right words. "What happened to keep you in prison for the maximum?"

"His family came to every parole hearing. His mama would tell the board what promise her son had. They even blew up the picture from the homecoming court and propped it up beside her." Janet took a long drink from her glass before she continued "Just seeing their name on the witness list each time, I knew I wasn't going to go anywhere for another couple of years."

"I don't think the Garretts ever believed that their son had harmed you."

"Well, I had a pretty hard time too believing I had harmed him," Janet responded.

"You never got your memory back about that night?"

"I tried so hard as I headed to trial. I thought if I could remember then I could make everyone see that it was a huge mistake." Janet finished shredding the mint sprig she had pulled from her glass of tea. "Afterward, it didn't seem that important."

"Did you ever see a counselor about that?"

"No, I didn't want to talk about it to anyone. Certainly not to a stranger that kept notes to share with the parole board." Janet's voice rose. She flushed when she saw the compassion in Sallie Lee eyes. "Talking about it wouldn't have gotten me out of prison any faster and might have made it even harder to bear. I couldn't risk it."

Sallie Lee shook her head sympathetically. "I think I can understand your reasons. Surviving was the most important thing."

"I got real good at that," Janet said bitterly.

"You got out two years ago... What have you been doing since?"

Janet shook her head. "I don't actually know."

"Explain that."

"It's hard." She massaged her temples with her fingertips. "See, I just sort of drifted. I would get work when I could. When I couldn't find work or was fired once they found out I was an ex-con, I would go somewhere else. I did a lot of walking."

"Is that how you ended up in Tupelo?"

She raised her hands in wonderment. "I don't know how I got into Mississippi. I was just there when I had the sudden urge to come back." She watched Sallie Lee go to the stove and baste the chicken again. "I was mopping the floor of this little restaurant and I couldn't breathe for the need to get out of there and back here."

Janet slowly swept the pieces of mint into a pile and then divided the pile into smaller sections. "I caught the first bus I could get that headed this direction." She scooped the mint up and carried it over to the trash can. "I made the mistake of falling asleep in the Birmingham bus station and woke up with my ticket missing. I ended up hitching the rest of the way." Janet pushed the hair off her forehead. "As soon as I got here, as soon as I saw the Veterans Memorial, the compulsion was gone. I don't know why it was so important to get to this place." She glanced up at Sallie Lee to see if she understood.

"Maybe Della was right that home was calling to you."

"Just getting back here wasn't at all like coming home, though. There is no there there."

"You know your Stein."

Janet shrugged again. "She speaks to this feeling I have of losing what you might never have had. I don't even have a home anymore."

"The building may be gone, but the one thing I've learned is it's the feeling and the people that make something a home." Sallie Lee put a trivet on the table. "When I first came home after college, I was so very angry. This place had never felt so confining. But, when I returned after cooking school, I felt free." She set out the plates and flatware as she continued to talk. "It's all in what we bring to it that makes it a home."

"You've done a lot to make this place welcoming."

"Thank you. You are welcome to make it your home." Sallie Lee appeared a little startled to hear that come out of her mouth.

Janet nodded, oblivious to the undertones of the offer. "I know I felt comfortable from the first moment I sat in your diner."

Sallie Lee smiled at her and handed her another sprig of mint. "You want to actually put this one in your glass?"

"I have more fun playing with it," Janet answered. "You don't mind?"

"If you consider ripping the poor thing to bits to be playing. I personally prefer peeling the labels off beer bottles when I'm nervous, which usually happens when I'm in a bar. I don't have to worry about the glass feeling pain." She smiled at her. "Just do whatever makes you happy."

"I don't think my happiness depends on the damage I can do to things," Janet laughed. "So, what about you? You seemed pretty happy to leave this town for school. I don't think I would have ever pictured you settling down here. Why did you come back?"

Leaning against the counter, Sallie Lee was silent for a long moment. When she started to speak again, Janet had to strain to hear her.

"I never expected to be back in this house. I chose a college in Virginia to get the hell out of this state and that was as far away as my parents would let me go. I fully planned to keep heading north in increments until I made it as far as I possibly could. New York City was my ultimate goal." Sallie Lee opened the oven to baste the chicken. "I came back about six months after I graduated from Hollins to take care of my mother. She went downhill fast after Dad had his final heart attack." Sallie Lee stepped over to the table and took a deep drink of her iced tea. "I was torn between wanting my own life and scared I was going to lose both of my parents in such a short period of time." She pulled back a chair and sat down. "Of course, it didn't help that no one else in the family offered or made the effort to come back to take care of her. I really resented my siblings for a while." She shook her head sadly and was silent for a few moments.

"Once Mama was gone, I had time and the means to figure out what I wanted to do with my life. When I was honest with myself I realized that some of my favorite memories were of this place." Sallie Lee looked over at her and her eyes were alight. "I loved this town even when I hated it for confining me. Coming in to the courthouse to see Dad at work and then us all going to have lunch together at Mama's Place."

Sallie Lee winked at Janet. "I enjoyed those meals. Your mama had such a great way about her. I can't replicate her light touch with biscuits and pies." She smacked her lips. "Although, you do a good job there, too. Anyway, I took my part of the life insurance and went to the California Culinary Academy in San Francisco to learn to be a chef and how to run a restaurant. I came home and bought your mother's old place. It had been standing vacant for a number of years so it was easy to convince the realtors to let me take it off their hands at a rock-bottom price. Took a loan from my brother Robbie to buy the appliances and, in the past year or so, have started to see black more often than red in the ledger."

Rattling the ice left in her glass, Sallie Lee smiled at Janet. "I do enjoy what I do. I don't think I can ask for anything else."

"So, you're happy?"

"You know, I think I am."

"How about outside of work?" Janet asked casually.

Sallie Lee stood up. "All this talk is making me hungry and thirsty. Let's eat."

"I'll get the salad," Janet offered.

The two of them ate in companionable silence. The only sound was the metal of their forks against the china as they scraped the bottom of their plates.

Janet cleared her throat. When Sallie Lee glanced up, she stated, "I have to ask. Are we just going to ignore that I asked about your personal life?"

"I wasn't ignoring you," Sallie replied with a bright smile that did not reach her eyes.

Janet scoffed, "And that's why you answered the question in a way that only the neighborhood dogs could hear?"

"I was hungry and seeing the condition of your plate, I see that you were too."

"I'm not arguing that, doll. Sheesh, forget I said anything." She picked up her fork again. "This chicken is really good," Janet stated as she chased the last bite of potato around. "You have my mom beat on the main courses."

"Thank you. I found I really like fusing different kinds of foods together. I sometimes feel trapped by the limited expectations of my customers."

"You could feed them exotic things if you call them by familiar names."

She looked askance at Janet. "How do you mean?"

"Well, how about empanadas? No one will eat them with that name but will clamor for pocket pies. Heck, even McDonald's serves breakfast burritos."

Sallie Lee laughed. "Yeah, it was strange to see that appear on their menu. I'll have to think about it."

"Let me know when. I want to volunteer to be a member of your tasting committee."

"Well, if you are always so generous with your praise, I'll have to for purely ego reasons." Sallie Lee carried her plate to the sink. She opened up the dishwasher and began to load it with the dinner dishes. "Where did you learn to cook?"

Janet rose as well and helped to clear the table. "Osmosis. I worked in the diner nearly every morning before school and on the weekends. Mom never really sat me down to teach me, I just did what I saw." Janet shrugged. "They had me in the kitchen in Tutwiler. The food there was high in starches—potatoes, rice and pasta. There wasn't much room for variety, but I was able to play a little with the menu after a while." Janet wiped the table and rinsed out the sponge. "Once I got out, I was able to find work as short-order cook wherever I went. I still remember a lot of the recipes my mom used to use."

"Hey, I didn't mean to snap earlier." Sallie Lee closed the dishwasher and leaned back against it.

"It's okay if you don't want to answer something." Janet smiled at her. "Given your tendency to ask me questions, I figured it was okay to ask a few myself."

"You can. I'm sorry."

"Don't worry about it."

"I'm a little sensitive about my decided lack of a social life."

"Did you think I would judge you?"

"No, that's not it. It's just, I think I have internalized my homophobia."

"What does that mean?" Janet asked, genuinely puzzled. "I thought you were a lesbian like me."

"I am. It's just that I haven't kissed a girl since college. Sometimes I think that I'm only a theoretical lesbian."

"Theory because you haven't had much practice?"

"Yeah."

"Am I supposed to tell you that it's like riding a bicycle?"

"If it is."

"Unfortunately, I'm not the best person to answer that. I have pretty limited experience to draw from," Janet responded apologetically. "Are you ashamed of who you are?"

"No! Not at all."

"Then why call yourself a homophobe?"

"Because I'm almost forty and I've never had a relationship that lasted longer than a tube of toothpaste. There must be something wrong with me."

"Well, you did bury yourself in a town with only two stoplights. How many gay people are even in Pennington?"

"The guys who run the antique mall by the highway."

"Anyone else?"

"Not to my knowledge. The only other ones I knew about left town after high school and never looked back."

"I don't think there is anything at all wrong with you. Beautiful, smart, funny, own your own business—in a town with any lesbians you'd be catch."

"You think I'm beautiful?"

Janet blushed. "I've got eyes, don't I?"

"Thanks. That's sweet of you."

"I wasn't just saying it to be nice. I think you should be proud of who you are and I'm sorry if my questions hit a sore spot."

"I think we're both going to have to accept that until we know each other better we're going to occasionally hit a land mine. I want us to make a pact that neither of us has to answer what we can't."

"I can agree to that."

"No matter how hard it is to say a thing, sometimes the things we say may be just as difficult to hear. Do you think you'll still be able to listen?"

"Courage is what it takes to stand up and speak; courage is also what it takes to sit down and listen."

Sallie Lee grinned. "Who said that?"

Distracted momentarily by the way the smile transformed Sallie Lee's face, Janet coughed and answered, "Winston Churchill."

"It's a good one."

"Amelia Earhart said that 'Courage is the price that life exacts for granting peace.'"

"You're just a regular Bartlett's aren't you?"

"I spent a lot of time in a small library. It was safe there." Janet looked up at Sallie Lee. The spotlights in the ceiling reflected off the few strands of silver in her long dark hair. Janet was drawn anew to the quiet strength that radiated from Sallie Lee. She confessed, "Before coming here, it was the only place I ever felt that."

"I'm so glad you found your way here. I hope we can continue to talk, too. I may get uncomfortable sharing some stuff but I promise to be honest with you."

Janet thought hard for another quote that might make Sallie Lee smile at her again. "'Honest men esteem and value nothing so much in this world as a real friend.' That one's from the fable writer Bidpai."

"Okay, now you are just being annoying." Sallie Lee put her hand on the light switch and ushered Janet out of the kitchen. "On a lighter note, I really need to drive up to Birmingham tomorrow. I need to see a man about buying a new car. Think you can handle breakfast on your own?"

"I'll do my best," Janet assured her. She remembered how hard she used to work as a doubles partner to never disappoint the older girl. Even now, she knew that she did not ever want to fail Sallie Lee. She would make the next day's solo flight in the kitchen a success if it killed her.

CHAPTER TWELVE

The ride to the café was quiet, the streets deserted in the early morning. The two women flipped on the lights and stood for a moment in the cool kitchen. Sallie Lee was a bit nervous about leaving her diner in someone else's hands but she was doing her best not to show it. Janet felt even more nervous at being left in charge of the cooking.

After the third time she tried to show Janet where she kept the bacon, even Della began to lose patience with her fussing. "Go on, get out of here."

"I just want to make sure she knows where everything is."

"Just go. Don't come back without a decent car that was made in this decade."

Sallie Lee left reluctantly and the two workers took a long

assessment of each other. They had not really spoken since Della had warned her off hurting her friend.

Placing her hands on her well padded hips, Della asked, "Are you all right?"

"Yes."

"You've done this before, right?"

"I can do this," Janet told her.

"You better," Della replied tartly.

Janet lifted her chin. "I'll need your help though." The admission came reluctantly but sincerely.

"I wasn't sure if you knew that or not."

"We'll both be in pretty bad shape if Lee comes back to find that we either killed each other or burned the place down."

"I'll do what I can," she promised. Reaching out her hand, Della asked simply, "Pax?"

"Pax." The two women shook hands.

Janet worked quickly and quietly all morning. During the few lulls, she started the prep work for the lunchtime meal, washing and tearing the lettuce for the salads, making the dressing, and reorganizing the counter with the hamburger patties out instead of sausage, and the grits got put away in favor of a large pot of mashed potatoes.

As the time went by, Della was impressed with how fast she worked. Orders were up in record time. While the two of them did not joke around as much, it was remarkably easy to work together.

The day went by in a rush and soon after they had locked the door behind the last customer, Sallie Lee returned from her shopping expedition.

"Was Bwana successful?" Della cracked.

"Yes, the great hunter has returned in Subaru style. Dark green. Air conditioning, of course, and cruise control. A six disc CD player. Not much else cool, remember, I did buy from what they had on the lot."

"Can we see it?"

"Of course. How about we take a ride around the block after we finish up here?"

Della rode around the block with them and then they

dropped her off at her car. Janet moved into the front seat for the drive home.

"This thing is boss, man."

"And that's a good thing?"

"Totally."

"Thanks, Jan. I want to thank you for your work today. I heard nothing but praise from Della and she heard it from a few of the lucky folks that enjoyed the lemon dessert."

"Thank you for trusting me with your baby. I know how hard it is for you to let go."

"You are very welcome. With the success of the tarts, I'm promoting you to pastry chef. I just hope the rest of your recipes stand up to the high expectations you set for yourself."

"Really? You're going to let me keep cooking?"

"Let you? Honey, I insist you do so." Sallie Lee winked at her passenger. "Now that I know how good you are, I can work on some of the other things that need doing like updating the menus and working on my business plan." She turned the car into the driveway. "I have plans for my place and you're giving me a way to get there."

They got out of the car and Sallie Lee walked around the vehicle. She removed a rag from her pocket and wiped off the windshield.

"How long are you going to obsess about that thing?"

"Until the first scratch, I reckon."

During dinner they talked about each other's day and then the conversation drifted toward each other's past.

"So, what part of San Francisco did you live in?"

Sallie Lee gazed at her through half-closed eyes before answering. "I lived in Noe Valley but spent a lot of time in the Castro."

"Mmhmm." Janet smiled knowingly.

"You haven't been out of the South in your life," said Sallie Lee. "What do you know of San Fran?"

"I was in prison, not a convent," Janet responded. "I know all about the friendly neighborhoods of the Gay Mecca."

"You know what I miss the most?"

Janet was intrigued. "No, what?"

"Hugging." Sallie Lee opened her arms. "I miss full-body hugs, when you fit together just right." She hugged herself. "Out here, you only get the upper body hugs. Or worse, the quick shoulder squeeze and air kiss. I miss pressing together from thigh to head."

"Do you want a hug now?" Janet asked her.

"Which kind?"

"I think you know which kind."

Sallie Lee looked over at her before she opened her arms again. Janet stepped to her and they moved against one another. Laying her head into the curve of Sallie Lee's neck, she whispered, "I had a crush on you in high school."

"I know. Julia Ann told me."

Janet stiffened, appalled at that revelation. "When did she tell you?"

"The summer you were sent away. She was devastated. When I came home for break, she told me everything."

Janet pulled out of her arms and backed up against the pantry door. "No, you're not serious. Not everything?"

Walking up to Janet, Sallie Lee cupped her face and kissed her lightly on the nose. "She told me about the time you two fooled around." Her face turned serious. "I think that's part of the reason she took the whole turmoil so badly. She was confused and then, suddenly, everything was so public."

"She wasn't talking to me at the time."

"Oh?"

"Yeah. We'd fought about her going to the homecoming dance with Jonathan. It was hard enough watching her and the other guys make out, but Jonathan was a Neanderthal." Janet bit her lip. "I could accept that she didn't want to be with me. It hurt but I understood she didn't have the same feelings. I just didn't see how she could choose those losers instead."

"The guy she married is pretty cool. They met at school and haven't been apart for more than a couple of days at a time since then."

"I never wanted to hurt her."

"I think she knows that now. She wouldn't talk about it for years but after Mom died she became a social worker at a rape crisis center." Sallie Lee tugged on Janet's bangs. "She knows all about not blaming the victim."

"I know all about being a survivor." Janet picked up the rest of the dinner dishes and loaded them in the dishwasher.

"Tell me, am I in any of your fantasies now?" Sallie Lee asked her.

Janet blushed prettily. "I won't answer that on the grounds that it may incriminate me."

"Chicken." Sallie Lee turned and flounced out of the kitchen. "Turn off the lights before you come upstairs."

"Goodnight," Janet called as she watched Sallie Lee ascend the stairs. The jeans she was wearing were tight in all the right places.

Sallie Lee turned at the landing and caught Janet checking her out. Smirking, she blew a kiss. "Pleasant dreams."

CHAPTER THIRTEEN

They were quietly sitting on the back porch one evening when Sallie Lee asked, "What was prison like?"

Janet did not answer immediately. She got up from the swing and paced to the front screen and back. "It was hard, no lie. Everyone telling you what to do every minute of the day. I thought my days were regimented outside with chores and school and stuff but that was nothing like inside." She continued to pace. "My biggest problem was learning to shower, eat, sleep and shit with all those people watching all the time." She glanced at Sallie Lee and flashed a quick smile. "I used to have a really shy bladder but I got over that awful fast."

She picked some dead leaves off the hanging spider plant, dropped them in the pot and dusted off her hands before she continued. "In prison you're faced with long stretches of boredom and minutes of sheer terror. There wasn't much to do but fuss with one another. I made a pretty good target."

Shaking her head, she said, "I was so clueless. When I got there, they put me in the area with other young adults. Man, the girls in there were tough. Most of them came up from the juvenile farm camps and were mean as snakes. Seemed they all had knives and just itched to use them." Janet turned and faced Sallie Lee. "I hadn't ever had to fight for anything before, much less for my food or even for my blanket. And it seemed like I was always doing something wrong, sitting in the wrong area, talking to the wrong person, walking the wrong way." She inhaled deeply. "I wasn't any good at fighting."

"You didn't even have anyone to fight growing up. Your brother was already in high school by the time you were out of diapers," Sallie Lee commented, her face soft with sympathy. "I can't imagine what it was like for you."

"I never knew that sibling rivalry had such a positive benefit." Janet sighed. "Just talking about it makes me crave a cigarette. I smoked all the time inside. That was about all you could buy at the store. That and chocolate. Anyway, once I got out, I couldn't see paying to kill myself, so I quit." She grimaced and held out her hand, two fingers extended as if there were a butt between them. "A filthy habit but at least it gave me something to do with my hands."

"Considering that you are currently using your hands to destroy my plants, I think I understand your craving."

"Sorry," Janet apologized. She stepped away from the planters. "Shall I go on?"

"Yes, please. I do want to hear about it."

"It wasn't until I got into the general population that I was adopted into a kind of family and didn't have to fight all the time. They got me working with them in the kitchen and took care of me." Janet was careful not to look over at Sallie Lee as she started to pace back and forth again. "I spent as much time as I could in the library, reading." She laughed shortly. "That was the only place I was safe." She turned to Sallie Lee. "I got my GED and a bachelor's out of it, so it wasn't all bad."

"It sounds horrible," Sallie Lee said. "I know anything I say would be inadequate but I am glad you survived."

Janet sat down on the swing and rubbed her eyes. "Sometimes I wonder why I did," she muttered.

"Because you had unfinished business you needed to take care of?"

"You believe that?"

"As much as I believe that you didn't deserve what happened to you. Don't for a minute think that anything you did made it okay for someone else to beat or rape you."

"Somebody died because of me!"

"Quid pro quo?"

"What?"

"It means an equal exchange. I was wondering if you think you would be better off dead?"

Janet stiffened angrily. Sallie Lee got up and stood next to her but not so close as to crowd her. "I'm sorry, honey. I didn't mean to push you so hard."

As her breathing calmed, Janet pushed her bangs out of her eyes. "I don't know what I think anymore."

"You think you might be ready for dinner?"

"No, thanks. I'm not really hungry."

"Nonsense. We covered some pretty heavy stuff tonight. You need some comfort food." She thought for a minute and snapped her fingers. "I know, how about some mac and cheese?"

"You're kidding?"

Sallie Lee looked affronted. "I never joke about food. Pasta is a mood lifter, too. How about we make some cheesy goodness and stay on lighter topics for the rest of the night?"

"Sounds good. Thinking back on it for too long tends to give me nightmares."

"We can't have that." Sallie Lee started a pot of water boiling. "I don't want my tendency to ask questions to cause you grief any more than I want my cooking to give you indigestion."

"Well, that hasn't happened yet."

Sallie Lee sighed dramatically. "Thank goodness for small favors."

Busying herself with a whisk, she concentrated on getting

the sauce together. She vowed to be a little more sensitive during their next chat and had to stop for a moment to savor the feeling of warmth she got in the pit of her stomach.

"What?"

Sallie Lee looked over at Janet in confusion. "Huh?"

"I was just wondering what the smile was about."

"Oh," she replied, blushing. "I was just thinking about getting to know you better."

This time it was Janet's turn to blush. "Me too," she answered. "This has been fun."

"Yeah. I've been enjoying the past weeks and I don't want them to end." Sallie Lee poked a finger at her houseguest. "But enough mushy stuff. I need you to finish with the grater so we can get this meal on the table."

Grumbling good naturedly, Janet followed her directions to the letter.

As she drifted off to sleep later that night, her thoughts were filled with future possibilities and not on the darkness of her past.

CHAPTER FOURTEEN

Standing in the doorway to the living room, Sallie Lee studied Janet. She was sitting in one of the big stuffed chairs reading *Zen and the Art of Motorcycle Maintenance.* Sallie Lee watched as the younger woman un-self-consciously pushed her bangs out of her eyes before she licked her thumb and turned the page.

In the short time since Janet had returned to her life, Sallie Lee had begun to realize how alone she had been. Thinking about the other important woman in her life, she was amazed at how much more at ease she was with Janet. She had always felt that she needed to be on her best behavior around her one and only serious girlfriend.

Susan had been from a well-connected Washington, DC family and had been initially charmed by Sallie Lee's small-town provinciality. She was also an unapologetic name-dropper and Sallie Lee never lost her feelings of being found lacking compared to the more famous people who littered Susan's intimate landscape.

She shook her head slightly. She was amazed at how comfortable she felt in her own skin around Janet. She also acknowledged that for the first time since the death of her parents the house felt like a home.

Sallie Lee brought out a shoebox of pictures to sort and put into an album. She sat on the floor in front of Janet's chair with the photos on the coffee table. She played with the pictures for a few minutes before she made up her mind.

"Look at this one," she said to Janet, tapping a photo of herself at age ten. Janet had to lean over her shoulder to see and Sallie Lee shook her hair out, partially blocking the view. She sat there, holding her breath until she felt the light touch of fingers in her hair, smoothing it back over her shoulder.

"You are so cute in taffeta," Janet acknowledged softly.

She settled back in the armchair and Sallie Lee immediately shifted back with a handful of photographs in her hand. At first, Janet's legs were closed behind her but they eventually opened, allowing Sallie Lee to nestle between them.

Sallie Lee shuffled through the deck of photos, flipping her hair out of her way and onto Janet's bare knees. After a few moments, she again felt the soft touch of Janet's fingers. Taking pleasure from the gentle strokes, Sallie Lee set the pictures down on the coffee table. She rubbed her head against Janet's hand like a cat, purring and begging to be petted. Janet's hand opened and she played with the long, black hair. She ran her fingers through it like playing with running water, and then stroked Sallie Lee's head from forehead to the nape of her neck. Each pass seemed to make the fingers surer of themselves.

After an enjoyable few minutes, Sallie Lee leaned her head back and looked up at Janet through half-closed eyes. She kept her eyes on Janet's lips and was rewarded by seeing them part. She smiled as Janet's fingers continued to explore her face.

Janet stroked the length of her throat and Sallie Lee's eyes closed in pleasure as Janet lightly ran her fingertips over her lips and eyes. Caressing her soft ear between fingers and thumb, Janet suddenly pinched the lobe with her fingernails. Sallie Lee's eyes opened in surprise and she looked into the laughing eyes of the woman for whom she was starting to have deep feelings.

"I wanted to make sure you weren't falling asleep on me," Janet murmured.

Sallie Lee forgot the brief pain as her smile answered Janet, who bent down to kiss her.

The kiss started slowly, Janet barely brushed Sallie Lee's lips with her own. Then her tongue quickly darted between Sallie Lee's parted lips. They began kissing with more force, with more tongue and gentle bites and hardly stopped to breathe.

After breaking apart from her, panting, Sallie Lee turned around and got on her knees. She ran her hands up Janet's legs, putting her thumbs on the inside seam of her shorts. When her thumbs met at Janet's crotch, she looked up and grinned devilishly. "I didn't think you were ever going to kiss me."

Her face suffused with pleasure, Janet closed her eyes and gripped the arms of the chair. Sallie Lee took hold of her chin. "Janet," she spoke quietly, waiting for the other woman to meet her eyes. When the brown eyes stopped darting around the room, lighting on anything but her, Sallie Lee leaned up and kissed her deeply. She kept kissing her until Janet's hands returned to their exploration of her body and slid up her sides to settle under the heaviness of her breasts.

"Mmmm," she murmured into Janet's mouth. When Janet's thumbs passed over Sallie Lee's already erect nipples, Sallie Lee gasped and tightened her hold on the back of Janet's head. She slowly moved her lips over Janet's face, kissing everywhere, marveling at the feel of Janet's soft facial hair under her lips and tongue.

The shrill ringing of the telephone shattered the quiet intensity between them. The two women broke apart and, for a long moment, just stared at each other.

As it continued to ring, Sallie Lee groaned, "The phone." She glared over at it. "Really bad timing."

"Go ahead and get it," Janet said, pushing Sallie Lee gently away from her.

"I don't think I can stand up," Sallie Lee replied. She got to her feet just as the harsh ringing finally stopped. She grinned back at Janet but her smile faltered as the other woman quickly stood up.

"I'm sorry. I don't think this is such a good idea." She tried to go by Sallie Lee but was stopped by a soft hand on her arm.

"Wait. Talk to me."

Janet rubbed her temples. When she looked at Sallie Lee, her eyes were filling with tears. "Please, let me go. I can't do this."

"Tell me why?" Sallie Lee begged.

"You deserve better."

"Then why don't I have better already?" Sallie Lee demanded angrily. "I am sick and tired of everyone telling me that. If you don't want to be with me, at least be honest about why and not put it off on my inherent saintliness."

Janet's hands were trembling. "I do want you. I want you so bad I ache." She dropped her gaze. "It isn't fair to you to start something I can't finish."

"You're a tease as well, then?" Sallie Lee challenged her.

"Look, just trust me when I say this is for the best."

"I don't believe it. Cliché one hundred and twenty-four for the evening."

"Please, Lee. Just let me go."

"Whatever you want," Sallie Lee called as she stomped into the kitchen. "You do whatever you want."

She banged the pots around as she continued preparation of some roasted tomato soup. She only calmed down after she splashed hot liquid on her arm when transferring everything to the food mill. While she stood at the sink with cold water running over her arm, she let her frustration go down the drain with the rest of the water. Once the burn was cooled down, she trudged upstairs.

Janet's door was partially open. She pushed it the rest of the way and observed her housemate in silence. Janet was sitting on the edge of the bed with her head in her hands.

Sallie Lee sat beside her on the bed and put an arm around her shoulders. At first she was stiff and tense but then Janet took a gulp of air. She suddenly leaned into Sallie Lee's warmth and started to cry.

"Shh. I'm sorry. I shouldn't have pushed you," Sallie Lee whispered into the top of Janet's head. She held onto the narrow shoulders as the sobs slowed down and faded.

Hiccupping, Janet pushed away from her and tried to speak. Sallie Lee put her finger on Janet's lips. "No, don't say anything. Come downstairs to dinner when you're ready."

"I'm sorry. I didn't mean to freak out on you."

"Let's not mention it again, okay?"

Sallie Lee stood up and pulled a tissue out of the box on the nightstand. "Wipe your eyes, honey. Let's just forget it ever happened."

She smiled at Janet as she turned and headed back downstairs.

Janet whispered, too faintly for her to hear, "What if I don't want to forget?"

CHAPTER FIFTEEN

The alarms went off too early for either of them the next day. Janet was first into the kitchen and she fiddled with the coffee pot until Sallie Lee walked in the room. She put a cup of coffee on the table for her and watched while Sallie Lee poured in half and half and began to stir.

"I should go," Janet stated carefully.

Sallie Lee had not slept well. She kept dreaming about the words, "I can't finish," and then waking to the memory of Janet's soft skin. "Don't even start that," she snapped at her. "I said last night to forget it. I mean it." Sallie Lee pulled a mug off the cup tree and handed it to Janet. "Please stay," she said softly.

Abashed, Janet stepped to the counter to pour herself a mug of French roast. She sipped it while quietly watching Sallie Lee's every move. There was a graceful economy of movement in the way Sallie Lee doctored her coffee to her satisfaction and moved around the kitchen, wiping counters and emptying the dishwasher. Even though the circles under her eyes testified to her poor night's sleep, she was not acting angry or frustrated.

Janet kept up her watchful attitude for the drive in to work. She was confused that Sallie Lee wanted her to stay even after she had behaved so poorly. Even now, all she could think about was the feel of her body under her hands.

Things were a bit strained as both women tried to navigate around each other in the small space of the diner. It did not help when Della came in to find the two women not talking to each other and hardly looking each other's way. It was evident to Janet that Della immediately jumped to the conclusion that Janet had done something to hurt Sallie Lee. It was nerve-wracking that every time Janet looked up, Della was glaring at her. Janet could not really blame Sallie Lee for not correcting Della's assumptions.

At the close of business, the two women returned to the Hybart house. The drive home was as quiet as the drive in to work.

After Sallie Lee set her keys down, she walked into the kitchen. Janet followed her and finally spoke. "I think I should leave," she repeated quietly.

"Look, I am not going to go through this with you again. You're welcome to stay here as long as you want. I want you to stay." Sallie Lee bit her lip. "Please stay. I'd feel really guilty if what I did made you leave."

"What you did?" Janet was puzzled. "I thought you were mad at me because of what I did or, more accurately, what I failed to do."

"No, I'm not mad at you. I'm pissed at myself for making you feel bad about not doing what you are obviously not ready to do." Sallie Lee walked to the refrigerator and pulled out small bag of key limes from the crisper. "I made a serious mistake last night. I assumed you were at the same place I was. I only know a little of your story but I should have known you weren't ready for the next step. I really, really want you to stay. Okay?"

She watched Janet until the other woman nodded. "Want

to take a walk?" she asked. "We could wander around the neighborhood."

"That would be nice."

The two women strolled along the tree-lined street. Magnolias, elms and oaks lined the wide avenue. Sallie Lee waved and called out greetings to her neighbors finishing chores on their lawns or sitting on their porches as the day cooled. Lightning bugs appeared and disappeared. The darkness closed around them, inviting them to share intimacies.

"I asked you a bunch of questions the other night," Sallie Lee said. "Is there anything you want to know about me?"

"Like what?"

"I don't know. I want you know that you are free to ask me anything."

"Okay. Um, when did you know you were gay?" Janet asked tentatively.

"I was afraid that I was gay in high school. But I didn't dwell on it because all I really wanted to do was play sports and so it was okay that I didn't date. I knew I was a lesbian my first semester of college. My roommate was already out and she would bring women to the dorm room. I got this strange tickle in my belly when I saw them kiss. I had the hots for all of them."

Sallie Lee batted a moth away from her face. "I didn't actually get to do anything until spring semester my freshman year. I pulled my back playing tennis and one of my teammates offered to give me a back rub."

Janet laughed. "The old 'Let me rub that for you' routine."

"It's only such a good routine because it works. Her fingers were marvelous and kept slipping farther and farther away from where it hurt to where it felt so nice." She shivered a little at the memory. "After that, it was like I was born anew. I couldn't get enough."

They crossed the street and strolled along the path that ran along the edge of the park. Sallie Lee stooped to pick up some acorns. She tossed them at the trees as they moved along. She smiled in satisfaction when every one that she threw hit its target. Skipping a couple of softball games had not affected her aim any. "I didn't really have a serious relationship until my senior year. I just had a real good time learning the joy of lesbian sex."

Janet grinned. "You were a slut puppy?"

"Hardly. I was serially monogamous, dating for the length of the semester and then breaking up. I fell hard for a woman completing her graduate fellowship at the United Nations." Sallie Lee wiped her hands on the seat of her shorts. "We only lived together briefly after graduation until my mom needed me. I couldn't ask Susan to give up her studies for me and she couldn't ask me to give up my family obligations."

Sallie Lee leaned confidingly close to Janet. "I was pretty much a homebody while Mom declined. I do regret that I never came out to her. Everyone else was cool when I came out to them. Julia Ann even said she knew from high school. That was why she told me about the two of you."

"What about when you were in San Francisco? There are plenty of wild women out west," Janet said, waggling her eyebrows.

"Hell, I didn't have time for anything when I went out to California," Sallie Lee retorted. "Cooking school was beyond full-time, with course work, labs and kitchen shifts. No, I stayed celibate, sublimating all my energies into food preparation."

After a few moments of silence Janet asked another question. "When you came back, what were things like?"

Sallie Lee picked up a blue jay's feather and twirled it between her fingers. "Same as before. I was busy with the restaurant. It's a lot of hard work getting a business up off the ground. I didn't have time for a life and I doubt I could have found anyone to share it in this town."

"I don't believe that. Remember, we are everywhere."

"Not in West Bumblefuck, Alabama," Sallie Lee responded.

"I get the feeling that everyone seems to know, though."

"That is one of the things I brought back from San Francisco," she said firmly. "I won't lie about who I am. If that means they don't eat my food, it's their loss. I don't want anyone to say I lived a lie."

"Truth to tell, we are all criminals if we remain silent."

"And who said that?"

"An Austrian Jew named Stefan Zweig. He escaped the Nazis by leaving Europe in 1934, but in despair over the war he and his wife committed suicide in 1942."

"Sometimes the obscurity of your quotes amazes me." Sallie Lee nudged her with her hip and Janet pretended to be knocked over. "Anything else?"

"Have you had any problems with being out?"

"Not really. In fact, it may have helped some. Most of the wives of the lawyers and city workers don't have a problem with their men hanging around my place since they know I am no competition."

They walked for several minutes in companionable silence. The cicadas were singing their summer song and making plenty of noise on their own. Sallie Lee looked over at the shadowy profile of the woman beside her. "What about you? What's your story?"

"My life is an open book."

"No, I don't think so. Tell me a story."

"Which one?"

"A personal one."

"The ones I have are not particularly pretty."

"I kind of figured that out when you seemed to gloss over stuff when we talked on the porch."

"Are sure you want to hear this?" Janet raised an eyebrow in question at her.

Sallie Lee put an arm around her shoulders and squeezed gently. "I want to know more about what happened to you. I want to know you better." She released her and they walked across the street. "But I also don't want to make you relive things that are uncomfortable for you. No pressure. You tell me what you want to."

"I don't have much practice talking about these things."

"Stick around for a while. I'll get you back in the habit." Sallie Lee smiled to herself. "I remember Julia Ann and you chattering away a mile a minute all the time. Nobody could get a word in edgewise."

"I lost that habit in prison. Didn't really have anyone to talk to and couldn't think of anything to say for a long time."

"What happened when you and Julia Ann fooled around?"

"We only kissed." Janet stressed the word only.

"You never tried again?"

Janet shook her head. "She joked about it, but I could tell she wasn't into it. She then went out and started dating those losers."

"Yeah, I remember my parents lecturing her on not settling for whatever the town could give her. They wanted her to wait before getting serious about any of the boys. Sometimes I wonder what my folks would say if they could see me now."

"I think they'd be proud. You are a successful entrepreneur."

"It's weird that I still need their approval."

"Nothing weird about it. Why do you think all those shrinks are in business?" Janet's voice took on a Germanic accent. "If it wasn't the mother's fault, zen it must have been zee distant father."

The two women reached the end of the cul de sac and turned back toward home. Sallie Lee snapped off a couple of sprigs of night-blooming jasmine and offered them to Janet. "What was your first time like?" Sallie Lee asked.

"I don't really remember much about what Jonathan did to me." Janet started to walk a little faster.

"You can't count that rape as a sexual experience. Rape is a crime of violence, not passion." She hurried to catch up with Janet. "For it to be sex, it must be consensual."

"Using that definition, I might still be a virgin."

"What? You haven't had sex?"

"The second night, after lights out, three girls came for me. I was lucky they didn't bring their toys. They generally liked to do new girls with broomstick handles." Janet stopped walking and stared down at her sneakered feet. "That was the first time I remember."

Sallie Lee reached out and took the almost crushed sprig from Janet's fist and laced their fingers together. "I'm so sorry," she murmured.

"It was actually an advantage to be in there for murder. People took you seriously." Janet pulled her hand free. "I wasn't much to look at either, so I wasn't a target for sex."

Sallie Lee cleared her throat. "I've watched a couple of women in prison films. You didn't hook up with anyone inside?"

"No. I never went with anyone from my choice."

Cocking her head at Janet's word choice, Sallie Lee asked, "What do you mean?"

"Ruth was the leader of the group that adopted me. She had the power to get things and she used several of us as currency. We all did what she said and that includes sleeping with who she said when she said it." Janet glanced at her. "So, in reality, I'm the slut."

"Oh, honey," Sallie Lee said sympathetically. "Did you have to do it a lot?"

"No. Enough." Janet's hand reached out for hers. "Like I said before, I'm not much of a looker."

Tightening her fingers, Sallie Lee grinned at her. "I find you quite easy on the eyes."

"Thanks."

They crossed the street before Sallie Lee spoke again. "What happened when you got out?"

"You mean romantically?"

"Yeah."

"I never stayed anywhere long enough to even consider getting involved with anyone." It was fully dark as they retraced their steps back toward the house. "Also, I'm not real comfortable with people touching me."

"You let me hug you the other day and we had a pretty fun snogging session until the blasted phone broke the mood."

Janet squeezed her hand. "I mean it when I say I am able to relax around you. I haven't ever been like that with anyone else."

"I feel honored." Sallie Lee tugged on her arm. "Don't let me push you into doing something you aren't ready for. I would hate to cause you further pain."

In the light from the porch, Janet's blush was easy to see. "I wasn't feeling any pain. I kind of liked it."

"Horrors. She only kind of liked it? Do you want to destroy my reputation?"

"I thought you'd been a nun since coming back here."

Sallie Lee drew herself up to her full height. "I was speaking of my reputation as the representative of the Lesbian Nation."

"Oh," Janet responded. "So, that's not just your wounded ego talking?"

"Keep laughing, young lady, and you won't get any sorbet."

"Yes, ma'am. I'll be good."

CHAPTER SIXTEEN

"I'm in the mood for a sundae," Sallie Lee announced two days later after they finished cleaning up after dinner. She pulled out the container of hot fudge sauce and waggled it at Janet. "Tempted?"

"Oh yeah. Load mine up."

They took their sundaes into the living room. Sallie Lee sat at the desk and shuffled through her mail. She got out her bankbook and wrote several checks. Janet picked up the book she started yesterday evening and curled up in the corner of the sofa to read. The house was quiet, except for the click of spoons against the bottom of the dishes.

Suddenly flooded by self-consciousness, Janet looked up to see Sallie Lee intently gazing at her as she sucked the remaining chocolate off her spoon. Blood rushed to her cheeks and she felt a stir of butterflies in her stomach.

"Your looking is like touching," Janet whispered.

"I'm not touching."

"Maybe, but I can almost feel you against my skin."

Sallie Lee got up from the desk and closed the distance between them. She sat down beside Janet and reached up to brush the bangs off her forehead. She then ran her fingertips across Janet's eyebrow and then her thumb across her lips. "Looking isn't enough. I want to touch you."

"Please," Janet murmured as she leaned toward Sallie Lee.

At first touch of their lips, Sallie Lee placed her hands on Janet's shoulders and pushed her slightly back. They caught their breath for a moment. Janet's face was flushed and her eyes were fixed on Sallie's lips.

"What's wrong?" she asked, looking confusedly into Sallie's eyes.

"I want to lie down with you."

Janet's breathing quickened even more and she nodded her willingness.

"Are you sure?"

Nodding again, Janet leaned forward to kiss her again.

Sallie Lee pulled back a bit. "Forgive me but I need to hear you say it."

"I want to be with you," she whispered.

"We will stop whenever you want," Sallie Lee assured her.

She took Janet by the hand and led her up the stairs and into the bedroom. She opened up her arms for Janet to step into the embrace.

They kissed again and held each other close. Sallie Lee bit Janet's lip and heard her gasp in surprise. She felt Janet's lips curve in a smile against her own as she kissed and licked the full, supple skin.

Janet pushed her back until, with steady pressure, she moved her down onto the bed. Janet nuzzled under her neck, licking and biting at the corner of her jaw and ear.

Janet sat astride Sallie Lee's waist. Sallie Lee sighed and raised her legs, bracing her feet on the covers. She stroked her hands along Janet's thighs and behind, to cup the full buttocks.

Janet stared down at the woman beneath her for a long moment before her hands unbuttoned the dress shirt. She gazed at what she had revealed. Sallie Lee's breasts were large and spread out and the areola around the nipples dark. Reverently, Janet leaned down and kissed the skin around her breast before flicking the nipple with the tip of her tongue. She then spread her tongue flat and pressed down on the nipple. At Sallie Lee's moan, she pulled back and blew lightly across the wet nub. The nipple tightened even further as Sallie Lee's grip on her ass tightened.

Janet teased both nipples, biting and licking and pinching and stroking with her fingers. Sallie Lee's hands fell to her sides and she convulsively clutched at the sheets.

"Please," Sallie Lee begged. Janet leaned forward and gently bit her neck. "Oh, God," Sallie Lee whispered, exposing her long neck even further. "Inside me, please."

Janet lay beside her. She glided her right hand up through the leg of Sallie Lee's shorts and, after one pass over her dripping clit, slid two fingers into Sallie Lee's warm cunt. She bit Sallie Lee's earlobe and asked in a whisper, "More?"

"Yes," she was answered. Janet introduced a third finger for a couple of thrusts. She then bunched all four fingers together and eased them in, resting her thumb against the hard nub of Sallie Lee's clit. She began to thrust slowly, letting her thumb ride back and forth. Sallie Lee was panting, her legs clenching and releasing as Janet thrust harder and faster before pulling out of her altogether.

"What...Janet?" she cried.

Janet painted Sallie Lee's breasts with her own juices and sat up. She grabbed both sides of Sallie Lee's shorts and pulled them off. She moved between Sallie Lee's legs spreading them wide before lowering her mouth to the tender fold of flesh. She had to hold the bucking hips down before being able to slide two fingers back into Sallie Lee's wet cunt.

"Please, don't stop," Sallie Lee moaned as she shuddered from the sensation of Janet's mouth on her mound. Her breathing quickened and her hips lost their rhythm as she began to come.

Janet crawled up Sallie Lee's body. She left her fingers inside the velvet channel being squeezed by the internal contractions. As the orgasm passed, she undulated the fingers without moving her hand. Sallie Lee's heartbeat and breathing increased and she came again before she had to reach down and pull Janet's hand from between her legs.

"Oh, sweet Jesus." Sallie Lee's eyes were closed. "I can't feel my hands." She lifted heavy arms and stroked Janet's face. She had a fuzzy smile on her face.

"Let me hold you," Janet said, enfolding her in her arms. "Just rest," she murmured as she hauled the comforter over them. She lightly trailed her fingers through her new lover's hair and listened to her breathing as Sallie Lee fell asleep.

Janet studied the woman beside her. As a teenager, she had dreamed about what had just happened. Tears welled up as she wondered why her dreams were being answered now. She cried silently, a skill she learned in prison, careful not to wake Sallie Lee.

It was completely dark in the room when Sallie Lee woke up. She stretched languidly before reaching out to find her lover. Janet had moved away from her to the far side of the bed. When Sallie Lee pressed against her, she stiffened. When she ran an investigative hand down along Janet's body, Janet mumbled a protest and tried to wiggle away.

Sallie Lee accepted Janet's subconscious response but left her arm across Janet's body. Breathing in the scent from Janet's hair, Sallie Lee fell back asleep.

CHAPTER SEVENTEEN

Sallie Lee slowly woke up the next morning and stretched like a cat. She was pleasantly sore in places that had not gotten a workout in far too long. Smiling to herself, she licked her lips and wondered if Janet was up for round two.

Reaching out one hand, she only felt cool sheets. She rolled over and opened her eyes, only to sit up with a grin when she saw Janet sitting at the end of the bed.

"Good morning."

The younger woman did not answer. Sallie Lee saw that she was wrapped in the blanket. "Is something wrong?" she asked.

Transferring her blank stare from her own knees to Sallie Lee, Janet asked, frowning, "Why would something be wrong?"

"You just seem upset or something."

"Or something is right."

"Are you mad?"

"Why should I be mad?"

"I don't have the foggiest idea. I thought we had a good time last night." Sallie Lee winked. "I know I sure did." When Janet did not respond, Sallie Lee's eyes widened. "Are you pissed that I fell asleep on you? I'm really sorry about that but you rocked my world and I couldn't help crashing after."

"No."

"Um, did I snore?"

Cocking her head, Janet replied, "No."

"Talk in my sleep? Hog the covers?"

"You think this is funny?"

"I don't know what to think. Tell me what is wrong!"

"You know why."

Sallie Lee raised her hands in surrender. "No, I don't. I don't understand what the problem is."

"Really? You think fucking last night fixes everything?"

"Whoa! First off, we didn't fuck last night. We made out together and then you made love to me. At least, I thought that's what we were doing." Sallie Lee felt her eyes fill with tears. "Please. Tell me what is bothering you."

"I can't believe you took advantage of me like that."

"*What*?"

"You know what happened to me and you still forced me—"

"Forced you? Like hell I did. Once we got up here, I never really touched you." Sallie Lee clutched the sheet covering her. "Yes, I led us to the bedroom but you took control once we were here."

"I wasn't ready."

"Janet, I don't know where you're coming from with this." Sallie Lee jumped out of bed and began to pace. "How can you think that of me?"

"So now I'm not allowed to think for myself? You have a pretty high opinion of yourself."

"I asked you if you were sure before we started anything." Sallie Lee shook her head. "I can't believe you'd accuse me of being a rapist." Pulling on her T-shirt, she glared at Janet's bowed head. "I've got to get some air."

Stomping to the dresser, she quickly put on jeans and shoes. She charged downstairs, grabbed her keys and drove the few minutes to the restaurant. Rocking the Subaru to a stop against the curb, she shoved it into park and walked with a heavy step inside.

Without a word to Della, she began the prep work for the day. The kitchen rang with the sound of pots banging. After the doors opened, Sallie Lee continued to take out her temper on the breakfast orders. The egg scramblers had never been so well stirred nor the buttons on the toaster harder pushed.

At ten o'clock, Della came into the kitchen and put her hands on her hips. "Okay, we're clear out front. How about you tell me what bug went up your butt?"

"Women! I don't understand 'em."

"Excuse me?"

"You heard me." Sallie Lee splashed a pot down into the soapy water and began scrubbing it with all her might. Water sloshed onto the floor and she snarled, "Who can fathom how their minds work? I sure don't."

"You sound like a guy."

"I can't help it. They are so freaking frustrating!"

Della laughed. "Okay, what did you do?"

"Me?"

"Yeah, you. You are sure talking like you did something boneheaded and are now trying to weasel out of responsibility."

"I'm not guilty of anything!" Sallie Lee pulled her hair with soapy hands. "I didn't do anything."

"I doubt that. No one is entirely innocent."

"What?"

Della smiled. "There are always two sides to every story. Tell me then, what did Janet do?"

"She's totally twisting what we had and making it dark and ugly."

"What you had? Oh ho! You dirty dog. You two got busy last night, didn't you?"

"Yes... No... Maybe."

"Okay, that's as clear as mud. Explain. Now!"

"We kissed and stuff for a while and then went upstairs."

Sallie Lee choked back tears. "It was so beautiful when I went to sleep last night and was all shit when I woke up this morning."

Della grabbed her arm and guided her to the nearest seat. "Okay, sit here and talk to me."

For a moment, Sallie Lee just sat at the counter, staring at nothing. Finally, she softly spoke. "She says I forced her."

"I can't believe you did anything of the sort. Think for a moment. Why would she say such a thing?"

"That's what I can't figure. I mean, she was a little stone but there was nothing traumatic."

"Stone?"

"Stone butch. It means someone who only gives and doesn't receive. They usually don't allow their partner to touch them back."

"Did she shut down? I mean, while you were doing it?"

"I don't think so. We cuddled after and I fell asleep."

"Okay, you need to go home."

"What? Why?"

"Because I'm not the one you need to be talking to about this."

"She didn't seem like she wanted to talk."

"Whether she did or not, you two need to discuss what happened last night and this morning. If you want my opinion, she just got scared. Instead of getting defensive, why don't you try being reassuring?"

"You want me to be all sensitive and shit?" Sallie Lee quickly got angry again. "I can't believe it. She's the one who owes me an apology. I didn't force her to do anything!"

"And unless you want to be single your entire life, you'll need to learn something pretty damn quick." Della rapped her knuckles on the counter. "When you're wrong, apologize. When you're right, keep your mouth shut."

"But—"

"Trust me. If you insist on being right and hearing an apology, you're not going to be in a relationship for long."

"That's not fair!"

Della laughed. "Nobody who has ever been in love would say that love is fair. If you want her and you to become anything together, suck it up and go home and talk to her."

Sallie Lee wiped her eyes and inhaled deeply. Holding it in for a moment, she finally nodded and exhaled. "Okay. Hold the fort. I'm going home."

The drive to her house seemed longer than usual but soon Sallie Lee was at her front door.

She stepped cautiously into the bedroom and saw Janet sitting on the floor, between the bed and the wall. "Hey," she whispered.

Lifting a tear-stained face, Janet blinked several times. "Oh. You came back."

"Of course."

"I thought…"

"What, Janet?"

"That I'd messed things up for us."

"No, you didn't. But tell me, what happened this morning?"

"I don't know. I didn't sleep well and I just felt so alone this morning. I don't know what I was saying."

"Next time, please wake me up. You are not in this alone and I'm not about to leave you now."

"I didn't mean it."

"Do you know why you said it though?"

"I don't. I was so confused and it scared me."

"Did what we do scare you?"

"No. I really liked kissing you and everything. It was nice." Janet paused and continued, "Really nice."

"I'm glad because I sure enjoyed it. Until the ambush this morning, that is."

"I'm so sorry."

"So am I."

"What? Why are you apologizing to me?"

"Because I reacted badly. We're both new to this and we have to give each other the benefit of the doubt. I just ran away." Sallie Lee opened her arms. "I could really use a hug right now."

Janet scrambled to her feet and shyly stepped into Sallie Lee's embrace. "Thank you for coming back."

"Don't worry, sugar. It's going to take more than an argument to keep me away from you."

The two women rocked against each other, bodies relaxing

together as the hug continued. Sallie Lee eventually leaned back a little bit and placed a kiss on Janet's forehead. "As much as I'd love to continue this hug and our conversation, we need to get into work."

"Della is all on her own?"

"Yeah and I'm afraid I may lose forever any customers she has to feed."

"She's not that bad." Janet giggled. "What is she going to say?"

"She already said a lot and that's why I came home when I did." Sallie Lee sighed dramatically. "Now I'll have to tell her she was right."

"She'll never let you forget it."

"I know. Let's get down there quickly so she can start gloating."

CHAPTER EIGHTEEN

It was just after eight o'clock the next morning when Ida Forest entered the diner. Her blouse was wrinkled and many strands of hair had escaped the tight, high ponytail. She stood for a moment breathing in the rich scents of breakfast. Sallie Lee was sitting at one of the tables working on her books. She looked up at the bell ringing and smiled openly.

"Well, what brings you here?"

"I need a fix of saturated fats, empty calories and carbohydrates."

"You came to the right place. Come sit here with me. Della will get you whatever you want."

With a heavy sigh, Ida sank into the seat. "Since when did she start cooking in your restaurant?"

"No, Janet is in the kitchen."

"Really." Ida raised an eyebrow.

Sallie Lee blushed. "Yeah, she's a good cook."

"Why do I have the feeling that food is not all she's been heating up?" Ida glanced up as Della approached wearing a brightly patterned gypsy skirt. "Darling, you are looking marvelous."

"Stop it. You'll turn my head." Della clicked her pen. "What can I get for you?"

"Hmm. For my first course, I'll have the bacon. I'll then have waffles and two eggs, sunny side and runny. I will need grits and some white bread toast, of course."

"Good thing you're a doctor. You'll need one if you manage to eat all that."

Ida appeared affronted. "It's good clean living that affords me the opportunity for the occasional indulgence."

"Whatever helps you get through the day," Della answered as she closed her pad. "Coffee and juice?"

"Yes, please."

"You might want to save some room for some of Janet's peach cobbler or plan to take one away with you for later. It'll be worth it."

"Mmm, dessert after breakfast. Now that is an idea that I can fully support." Ida poured some sugar into the mug of coffee Della brought her. "How are things?" she asked.

Sallie Lee hit the total key and wrote the figure down in the ledger. She grinned at her friend. "Black is beautiful."

"That's one thing you don't have to tell me." Ida raised her hands and clapped quietly. "What is this, one full year of positive cash flow?"

Sallie Lee nodded. "In one month it will be." She pulled her papers out of the way of the plates of food that Della brought to the table. "You know things are right when your tax preparer smiles when he sees you."

"How is Howard?"

"Still slick as a snake oil salesman." Sallie Lee sorted a stack of receipts. "He's done all right by me, though. Being a small business owner is scary sometimes. Navigating all the rules and regulations of the IRS code is more than I want to do alone."

Making a big production of the amount of food ordered, Della took two trips to serve the eggs, bacon, waffles, grits and toast.

Ida ate for a while, regarding Sallie Lee watchfully as she reconciled her books. "Talk to me."

"Pick a subject."

"How about that girl of yours. She seems to be settling in pretty well."

Sallie Lee nodded and stole a slice of bacon off Ida's plate. "Things are going pretty well."

"Going well here and at home?"

Sallie Lee snapped her head up. "How did you know that?"

"A little bird told me."

"Let me guess. A state bird?" Sallie Lee glared at the back of her waitress and business partner as she took an order from another table.

Ida reached for the syrup container. "My lips are sealed." She looked seriously at Sallie Lee. "I know your people move in together on the second date but this still seems awfully fast."

"My people?"

"Yeah. The U-Haul crew."

"Not all of us move that fast."

"Yeah, some of you have them move in before anything happens."

Sallie Lee glared at her. "I don't think I care for the direction or tone of this conversation."

"Don't get your panties in a wad. I am your doctor and your friend, Lee. I'm allowed to take your pulse."

"I don't know what to tell you, Ida. It feels like I've known her forever."

"She seemed depressed to me at the clinic. Are the indicators there?" Ida smacked at Sallie Lee's hand as she reached for a slice of bacon. "I'll stab you with my fork if you try that again."

Wrinkling her brow, Sallie Lee asked, "What indicators?"

"How is she sleeping?"

"Uh, not that well but her ribs have been hurting her."

"Is she restless or tired all the time?"

Sallie Lee nodded. "Yeah. Both actually."

Ida soaked up some syrup with her bread. "Does she act sad or express feelings of hopelessness?"

Sallie Lee's eyes got bigger. She asked, "Just how many signs are there?"

"Let's see." Ida counted on her fingers. "I haven't asked about her appetite, if she exhibits low self-esteem or has trouble making decisions. And the biggie, has there been any talk of suicide?"

Shaking her head, Sallie Lee grew concerned. "I can't answer those questions. Do you really think she might try to kill herself?"

"Ask her. More than likely she will answer you." Ida pushed her food plate to the side and pulled a ramekin with peach cobbler closer. "If she does, you need to encourage her to get professional help. Healing her is not something you can do by yourself." Reaching across the table to tap her index finger against Sallie Lee's forearm, Ida stressed every word. "Believe me when I tell you this. You cannot take responsibility for any action she takes."

Sallie Lee stared at her hands. "My head hears you but I'm not so sure about my heart."

"Hey, I'm hoping I'm completely off base here. Anyone who can do a better cobbler than my Gramma should have plenty to live for." She licked her spoon. "Della!" she called.

"Yes?"

"Give my compliments to Janet. This cobbler is terrific."

Della tugged on her bangs. "Yes, ma'am. Nothing would please me more."

"How do you put up with such cheeky help?" Ida asked.

"She is a good part of the reason we are doing so well. I don't know how she's able to convince folks to buy more than they normally would and it's more than just offering fries with every order. I don't know what I'd do without her."

Ida fished out her wallet from her voluminous purse. "So tell her. Everybody needs to hear they're worthy occasionally. I will see you at the game, right?"

"Yeah."

Sallie Lee and Della watched her walk out of the diner. Gathering up her papers, Sallie Lee asked her friend to cover the front for a minute. She went into the kitchen and saw Janet elbow-deep in sudsy water.

"Hey."

"Hey, yourself. Are you done with your paperwork?"

"Enough for now. Look, I need to ask you a question."

Janet dried her hands. "Okay."

"Tell me honestly. Did you come back here to die?"

Janet stood stock still and gaped at her. "Where did that come from?"

"Something Ida said." Sallie Lee put her hands on her hips. "Are you depressed?"

"I don't know."

"At least give the question some consideration before you answer it," Sallie Lee snapped. "This is important to me."

Janet looked contrite. "I don't know what it means. Sure, I get sad sometimes. Is that depression?"

"All right. Let me ask you something else. Why did you come here?"

Smoothing her apron, Janet paced back and forth. "I told you. I felt like I had to."

"Do you think about dying?"

"Sometimes, sure."

"Would you kill yourself?"

Looking up at her, her dark eyes somber, Janet shook her head. "I thought about it a lot when I was first in prison. I guess I didn't do it because I wanted more."

"Like what?"

"I'm not sure. I wanted out of the mess I was in but I couldn't bring myself to actually end my life." Janet continued to pace. "I felt the same urge once I was out."

"Why?"

"There wasn't anything for me out here." Janet waved an arm. "Everything I had ever known, everyone I ever loved was gone. I felt invisible wherever I went. As an ex-con nobody wanted to rent to me, or give me a job or even meet my eyes." Janet wrung her hands together. "I came back because I was a person here once." She clenched her hands into fists. "But there is nothing for me here, either."

"What do you mean? What about us?"

"Us? You can't seriously believe there is an us?"

"Why not?"

"Because I've only known you a couple of weeks."

"I think a week is plenty long enough to know," Sallie Lee remarked and then looked at Janet. "Besides, we are not talking about a week. You can't deny that we have a history. I knew you before. We practically grew up together."

Janet shook her head. "You can't believe that matters?"

"Yes. I believe that something or someone brought you back into my life."

"Really?"

"Yeah, I do. I also know that even if we didn't have any past at all together, we would have ended up together."

"How so?"

"I had a temperamental Italian pastry instructor in San Francisco. He stood weeping in front of our entire class speaking passionately about *un colpo di fulmine*."

"What is that?"

"Love at first sight."

"Unbelievable. You're a romantic."

"Yes, I am. I believe in romance and hearts and flowers and violins. I believe in the possibility of forever and I believe in you." Sallie Lee stood in front of her. "Since you came back into my life, I've started dreaming in color."

"That's just your imagination talking," Janet said but her face had softened.

"No. It is as real as what you are to me. I've held you in my arms. Seen you bleed." She reached out a hand. "I can't tell you any truer than you are alive and I am glad for it."

"I don't know what you're glad for. I'm a thirty-five-year-old who's spent almost half my life in prison."

"That's right. Fifteen years. But, Janet, you can't let them take your entire life. You've got a lot of living left. Don't give up on the rest of it because you had a bad time."

"A bad time! You think I'm through with everything just because I had a bad day?"

"I meant that—" Sallie Lee started to say.

"Sometimes I don't want to be alive." Janet sank to her knees. "I killed a man. My parents are dead because of me. My only brother is dead to me." She angrily dashed the tears from her eyes.

"What is your almighty rush?" Sallie Lee demanded. "Why are you so hell-bent on joining them?"

"Why am I alive and they are not?"

"I don't know what to tell you. But isn't that God's decision? She hasn't seen fit to bring you to heaven. Maybe she thinks you've got some more living to do."

"Don't you think I've caused enough pain to the people around me?"

Sallie Lee sat on the floor in front of her. She took one of Janet's hands between both of hers. "Let me tell you about this ancient Egyptian thing that I think is pretty cool. The gods of the dead perform a 'weighing of the heart' ceremony to judge whether a person's earthly deeds were virtuous. The jackal-headed god Anubis oversees a total of forty-two gods who listen to the negative confessions of the deceased." Sallie Lee released Janet's hand so she could talk with hers.

"See, they have to testify that they're innocent of crimes against the divine and community social orders. The person's heart is then placed on a scale, counterbalanced by a feather that represents Maat, the goddess of truth and justice." She held both hands out with one hand out in a fist and the other holding an imaginary feather.

"If the heart is equal in weight to the feather, the person is justified, basically without sin and achieves immortality. If not, the goddess Amemet devours it. That means the person would not make it to the afterlife.

"I think we have to earn our eternal reward. We have to justify our existence to some higher power." Sallie Lee brushed a strand of hair off her forehead and studied Janet carefully. "Do you really think you are ready to do that now?"

Janet cradled her head in her hands. "I'm just so tired."

"Maybe that's why you came home. To rest and recover. Not to die." Sallie got up and stretched her legs to relieve some of her anxiety. "Do you think that could be so?"

"I came back thinking I could just come home again and everything would be all right," Janet said through her hands.

"What exactly were you looking for?"

"I'm not sure."

"Think about it. What did you hope would happen?"

Janet took her hands from her head and shoved them into her back pockets. "I wanted a new start." She blinked. "I want to live," she said, surprise evident in her voice.

Opening her arms wide to embrace the entire room, Sallie Lee asked, "And haven't you found that, here?"

"I think I've found it with you." Janet looked into Sallie Lee's eyes. "It scares me to death how important you are to my well-being."

Sallie Lee said gladly, "Stick around, darling. The best is yet to be."

CHAPTER NINETEEN

Sallie Lee rocked back on her heels and wiped her arm across her sweaty forehead. She was working in the garden, weeding the vegetable beds while Janet worked the morning shift at the restaurant. Her phone rang.

Tugging off her gloves and looking at the caller ID, Sallie Lee was smiling when she flipped it open. "Hey, sister-mine. Long time, no hear."

"You know this whole phone thing works both ways, right?"

"True." Sallie Lee laughed and walked over to a rocking chair on the back porch. "So what's happening in HotLanta?"

"Not much. The kids and everyone are fine." Julia Ann paused. "Was there something happening there that you wanted to tell me?"

Sallie Lee sucked in a breath. "Who?"

"Carla Wilson sent me an e-mail."

"Ah. She and the other ladies from the Women's Club stopped by the other day."

"Yeah, she was happy to tell me who she saw working there with you."

"Janet came back into town about a month ago."

"And she's been staying with you."

"Yeah." Sallie Lee rubbed her eyes. "Is that a problem?"

"I don't honestly know."

There was a tone in her sister's voice she could not identify. "I thought you were over this town and all that went down here."

"I thought I was too. It's hard for me to admit that it upset me when I first heard."

Sallie Lee cleared her throat. "It might be more than just her working at the diner."

"Oh?"

"She's been more than just living here."

"Really?"

"Yeah. What do you think about that?" Julia Ann was quiet for so long that Sallie Lee strained to hear her breathing. "It's okay if you don't want to talk about it."

"No, that's why I called you." Sighing, Julia Ann said, "She was my best friend for as long as I can remember but that summer still hurts to think about. I wouldn't wish a prison sentence on my worst enemy and she was never that. Part of me is glad she's being taken care of."

"But?"

"Another part is mad that you're taking her side."

"What?"

"I know it sounds foolish but I almost feel like you're choosing her over me."

"That's never going to happen. No matter what happens between her and me, you're my sister."

"What do you mean, what happens between you two?"

Sallie Lee pulled at a fistful of hair. "I didn't do this to hurt you."

"Do what exactly?"

"We've kissed and stuff."

"Seriously? I knew she had a crush on you as a kid but I thought you didn't like her."

"I thought you both were annoying but she's not like that anymore. I mean, she can be annoying but she's also smart, funny and easy to be with."

"So you like her?"

"I do."

"You're not taking advantage of her, are you?"

"What do you mean?"

"She wanted you. I know that was flattering when you were still in college but there's been a lot of water under that bridge."

"I know," Sallie Lee whispered.

"What else?"

"What do you mean?"

"I don't know. Just the way you sounded just then. There's something else."

Pinching the bridge of her nose, Sallie Lee said, "She was damaged inside."

"She was damaged going in. Jonathan hurt her so bad she had to block out what happened. Who knows what else she's blocking."

"I don't think she hurt him. Or anyone else."

"I'm not saying she did. You forget I was there for the trial. There is no way she did anything considering how badly she was beaten. It never made sense that she got convicted."

"She said the Garretts were at all her parole hearings. Maybe they pulled strings at the trial."

"Who knows? Southern law has rarely been about justice." Julia Ann sighed. "That wasn't the first night the lights went out in Alabama."

"Cute."

"But what about what happened to her in prison?"

"She had to use her body as currency."

"That's unfortunate."

She was angered by Julia's casual tone. "That's all you can say? I would've thought all that social work training would have helped you form a more suitable response."

"No, I meant that it is going to be hard for you to know that she isn't still doing that. I know she didn't have a lot of experience before…"

"Not a lot?" Sallie Lee snorted. "Try none."

"I know. It means what she learned in there is all she knows. If you get involved with her, you'll have to be constantly confirming that she's doing only what she wants to do physically and that she's always there mentally."

"I know."

"I'm not sure you do. We've talked before about surviving sexual assault. The work isn't just done by the victim. It is hard on the friends, family and especially those intimate with them."

"I'm finding that out."

"If this is what you really want, you know I'll support you."

"You mean that? You'll be okay with it?"

"Lee, you deserve to be happy. God knows she deserves a little happiness."

"What about you?"

"Getting free of that place did a lot but the home I've made here has done more. I'm not going to pretend it won't be a little weird for me for you to be with her but I can get over it."

"Thanks, little sister. I was worried about your reaction."

"How worried?"

"Huh?"

"I just wonder if my disapproval would change your mind about wanting something with her."

"No, it wouldn't stop me."

"Good. I'd have my doubts about it if it did." Julia Ann giggled. "You know, you've been alone forever. Are you sure you remember how to do this?"

"Brat!"

"Seriously, though, Lee. Don't move too fast. If you're in for the long term, let it build at her pace."

"I hear you."

"Good. Know that I'd be happy to hear from you if you need to talk."

"Thanks. That means a lot." Sallie Lee leaned back in her

chair. "And I won't just wait for there to be an issue for me to call. I've missed our chats."

"Me, too."

"So tell me, what else is new with you and yours?" Letting the chair rock forward, Sallie Lee settled down to catch up with her sister's life.

CHAPTER TWENTY

The three figures were indistinct. They towered over her menacingly, and she could not make her arms or legs move. Suddenly, they were surrounding her and holding her down. She fought them and thrashed against their hands. In terror, she watched their teeth turn into fangs and their hands into claws. She felt the weight of them beside her as they tried to tear her legs apart.

"Janet! Janet, wake up!"

The figures were shaking her now and she freed one arm and was able to bat at them. Her hand connected with strange solidity.

"Janet!"

Her eyes flew open. Sallie Lee was leaning over her. "You're safe. It's okay."

Janet just stared at her while dragging deep breaths into her lungs. "Lee? What are you doing here?"

"I came in when I heard you call out."

"Did I hit you?" she asked in a husky whisper.

"Don't worry about it. I'm not going to take it personally."

"Sorry." She sucked in another deep breath. "That was one of the bad ones."

"Do you want to talk about it?"

"I want to forget about it." She pressed the heels of her hands into her eyes. "Did I say anything?"

"Not really words. You just yelled out." Sallie Lee cocked her head. "May I get in there with you?"

Janet held the covers up and Sallie Lee slid into the bed. "What now?"

"Let me hold you?" Sallie Lee asked as she pulled the comforter over them both. She moved closer but stopped before touching her.

Janet lifted her head so that Sallie Lee could slide her arm around her shoulders. She stared at the ceiling for a few moments before she rotated into Sallie Lee's embrace. She clutched Sallie Lee's T-shirt tightly in her fist, breathing fast. "I don't know what you want," she said desperately.

"I want you to try to relax." Sallie Lee's voice was low. "This is not a test."

After a while, Janet's tight grip released and her breathing deepened. The sound of the steady heartbeat beneath her ear calmed her further down. She was almost asleep when she felt Sallie Lee begin to stroke her hair.

The touch was soothing and arousing at the same time. She could not resist the urge to tip her head up and taste Sallie Lee's neck. Her skin was delicious and she licked along Sallie Lee's pulse point before kissing along her collarbone.

Janet barely tensed when she felt Sallie Lee gently tugging on her T-shirt. The feel of Sallie Lee's hot palms against her bare back made her start to tremble. Only the slow and steady trails that Sallie Lee's fingers drew from her shoulder to the curve at the small of her spine calmed her again.

As soon as Janet relaxed, Sallie Lee caressed with her fingernails. Janet gasped at the sensation that transferred the tingling on her skin to a throbbing of her center.

Without a word, Sallie Lee tugged Janet's hips until Janet was resting fully on top of her. Janet looked down at Sallie Lee beneath her. "Can you breathe like that?"

"You are hardly more than skin and bones. Try to relax and enjoy this."

"Oh, I am," Janet purred as Sallie Lee went back to stroking her fingers along Janet's back and sides. She felt herself melting into Sallie Lee's body as those fingers wandered farther, running down the outside of Janet's hips.

Janet brought her mouth to Sallie Lee's and got lost in the act of kissing her. She could not help tensing when Sallie Lee's hands brushed across her buttocks. When the hands kept moving down to her legs, Janet relaxed into the massage.

As the kissing and teasing touches continued, Janet could not help opening her legs and straddling Sallie Lee's legs. She needed more and whimpered as she pressed her hard clit against Sallie Lee's thigh.

The kisses became more frantic for a few moments as Janet tried to get even closer. She resisted a bit as Sallie Lee lifted her hands to clasp her head.

"Easy. Go slow," Sallie Lee murmured as she deliberately kissed Janet's jaw and eyelids.

"I want...I want more."

"You'll get more, baby. There is no rush."

Janet touched her forehead to Sallie Lee's and let her breathing return to normal. "You take good care of me."

"And I hope to take even better care shortly."

Janet drew in a quick breath as she felt Sallie Lee's fingernails stroke down her back to the sensitive skin of her upper thighs. Automatically, Janet opened her legs wider.

"That feels good. You are so hot and wet."

Janet stopped moving for a moment but continued when she felt the pressure of Sallie Lee's hands on her ass.

"Keep going, baby. This is so sexy. Do you feel me touching you?"

Janet nodded frantically. "Please don't stop."

"I don't want to stop. I want to keep touching you." Sallie Lee flicked her thumbs against Janet's hard nipples.

Moaning, Janet arched toward the contact.

"I know you are ready. I can feel your juices on my leg. Please let me touch you."

Janet was struggling on top of her. "Yes. Please."

"Stay with me now. Stay with the feelings that my fingers bring you."

Janet's body was awash with sensation as Sallie Lee pinched her breasts and then brushed her hands over the goose bumps that rose up all over Janet's skin in response.

"Please let me in," Sallie Lee asked as her fingers once again neared the cleft between Janet's legs.

"Yes. Oh, yes, please," Janet whispered.

"Good. Now, sit up."

Blinking, Janet stared at her. "What?"

"Trust me, baby. Come on," she requested as she tugged on Janet's biceps.

Janet moved slowly until she was kneeling above Sallie Lee's stomach. Sallie Lee reached up and lightly pinched Janet's nipples before she stroked her hands down to the dark curls. "Lean back," she whispered. "Brace your hands on the bed behind you."

Janet complied and Sallie Lee was able to insert one hand between their bodies. She then ran her other hand over the muscular legs. "Oh, you are so slick," she breathed. "My fingers are sliding around. Can you feel them? Do you want me to keep going?"

"Please," Janet begged. "More," she added as her hips moved involuntarily.

"Okay, baby." Sallie Lee pressed the heel of her hand against Janet's mound, letting her fingers press lightly against the tight opening to her vagina. "Do you want me to try to go inside?"

"Oh," Janet breathed. "I don't know."

"Can I try?" Sallie Lee pressed gently.

Janet almost groaned. "Yes. Try. Please."

"I will, baby, but I will stop as soon as you want me to." Sallie Lee slowly pressed one finger into Janet's hot core. She rubbed her thumb lightly on the hard bud of her clitoris and smiled when Janet's vagina opened in response. "I'm pushing my finger inside you. You are so warm and tight."

Janet's eyes closed as the feelings overwhelmed her.

"Look at me." Sallie Lee's voice was husky.

Janet struggled to focus on the beautiful body beneath her. When she looked at Sallie Lee's face she was immediately lost in the depths of her lover's eyes. Those eyes were filled with promises. Every fiber of her being wanted those promises kept.

Her hips were moving and she tried to bring more of her sensitive flesh in contact with those questing fingers. "Please."

"Do you like this?" Sallie Lee asked as she developed a rhythm with her finger sliding in and her thumb sliding over. "I know that I like doing this to you."

Panting, Janet cried out, "I can't hold myself up." She was trembling with need.

"I want to taste you," Sallie Lee said, tugging her up.

Janet shuddered in response to her words. "Lee, please." She could not ever remember being this turned on.

The feel of Sallie Lee's free hand on her lower back kept her grounded. Otherwise she would have leapt straight up in the air at the first touch of Sallie Lee's lips and tongue on her erect clit. Janet trembled as attention was lavished on her outer lips and a tongue lapped up her wetness.

Sallie Lee murmured, "You taste so good. I could stay here forever."

Struggling to stay upright, Janet gripped the wood headboard for support. "Please." She looked down into Sallie Lee's eyes. "Please."

Sallie Lee moved her thumb so that there was constant pressure on Janet's clit. "Tell me, baby. You say please. Do you want me to stop or do you want more?"

"More. I want... I need... I don't know."

"It's okay, baby. I want to make you feel good." Sallie Lee stretched her arm up and squeezed one of Janet's nipples between her fingers. "Does this feel good?"

"Yes. Very good."

"I'm glad. How about this?"

Janet hissed as she felt Sallie Lee alternately stiffen and relax her tongue as she licked up and around the folds. "Yes. Right there."

Amazingly, Sallie Lee increased the rhythm of her tongue and matched its movement with pinches on Janet's nipples.

"Don't stop." The whispered plea sounded desperate. "Please, Lee." The movements of Janet's hips lost coordination as she climaxed.

Sallie Lee held Janet up as her release undid her. "Shh, darling." Sallie Lee cradled the shuddering woman in her arms. "I've got you."

Janet cried, "I never knew it could be this much. You made me feel more than I ever have in my entire life."

"I know, honey. I feel the same way."

CHAPTER TWENTY-ONE

"Up and at 'em."

For a brief moment, Janet could not comprehend the words. Her brain had a hard time translating them into a language her post-coital body could understand. She was first aware of her nakedness. Her entire body blushed as she wakened to the wonderful soreness of her breasts and the lingering tenderness between her legs. She sat up in shock and gaped open mouthed at a fully dressed Sallie Lee.

"Hmm. Not exactly the reaction I was hoping for."

Janet stared at Sallie Lee and remembered everything that happened last. "You're still here." Her voice cracked on the last word.

"Of course, I am." Sallie Lee sat down on the bed beside her. "Honey, talk to me."

"You, uh, still like me?"

"Like you? Sugar, I've never tasted anything as good as you."

Janet blushed. She pressed her palms against her burning cheeks.

"My, god, you are so beautiful." Reaching out, Sallie Lee ran her fingertips over Janet's ear and down the line of her jaw. "I really enjoyed last night and look forward to a chance to put the practice back in practicing homosexual."

Looking at her through her eyelashes, Janet nodded and said, "I'd like that."

"Glad to hear it. Now, you need to get up and take a shower. I really don't want to give Della any more ammunition."

Grinning at the memories of the night before, Janet quickly showered and got dressed. She ran down the stairs three at a time.

"Whoa. Don't break your neck."

"Sorry."

Sallie Lee shook her head. "If you don't wipe that silly grin off your face, Della is going to tease you unmercifully."

"She won't tease me." Janet slid into the passenger seat. "She'll tease you."

Resting her forehead on the steering wheel, Sallie Lee groaned. "I'm not sure how in the world I am going to get through this day."

"To start with, it will help if you put the key in the ignition."

Sallie Lee drove them into work. Della took one look at Janet's face and began to grin delightedly. Janet felt like her face would be permanently frozen in a blush.

It was late in the day when Sallie Lee cleared her throat. Janet looked up from restocking the refrigerator from the freezer.

"I want to invite you out to dinner."

"We have dinner every night."

"No. I mean a real dinner in a fancy restaurant with tablecloths on the table."

"I can't afford fancy."

"I am inviting you out on a date. Your only responsibility is to order expensive items off the menu and contribute sparkling conversation." Sallie Lee blew some sudsy bubbles at her. "What do you say? You want to go on a date with me?"

Janet nodded. "I've never been on a date before. What do I need to do?"

Della walked in on the conversation. "What do you need to do when?"

"Lee is taking me on a date. I don't know how."

"Oh, sugar, you have come to the right woman. Come with me, dear. Aunt Della will tell you all you need to know."

Sallie Lee looked at the two of them walking out of the kitchen. "I have a bad feeling about this," she muttered.

Even though Sallie Lee badgered her during the rest of the close procedures, Janet refused to divulge anything that she discussed with Della. Sallie Lee tried to wheedle it out of her on the drive home but Janet proved remarkably deaf to her pleas.

"I do need to borrow some clothes. I don't think I have anything that would meet the dress code of a place with tablecloths."

"Not a problem. Why don't you check out my closet while I take a quick shower?"

"What are you going to wear?"

"I have this darling black silk shirt that I have been waiting for a chance to wear."

Janet saw the movement of clothes to the ground out of the corner in eye and she turned to see Sallie Lee stripping off her clothes. She stared at the naked body of her lover. Sallie Lee posed in front of her for a moment before she turned around and headed into the bathroom. It was not until she stepped out of sight that Janet remembered to breathe. Once the water started, she blinked and reached into the closet for a pair of dark green chinos. She took her find into her room to get ready.

Stepping into Janet's bedroom after her shower, Sallie Lee finished screwing on the back of her earring. She stood close to

Janet who was staring at her reflection. "So, tell me what happened this morning when you woke up." She placed one hand on Janet's shoulder and the other teased her lover's belly button.

"I remembered coming and crying. I thought you would be upset with me." Janet arched as searching fingers slid past the waistband of her slacks.

Sallie Lee's voice was husky. She touched her lips to the curve of Janet's ear. "I am so grateful that you were able to climax for me." Her tongue darted out to lightly lick the warm flesh. "You are safe here. You can cry whenever you need." She ran her tongue over the soft skin behind the jaw. "I like that you get so wet for me," she continued as her fingers slowly eased past the barrier of Janet's panties.

Groaning, Janet turned her head and captured Sallie Lee's lips in a hungry kiss. Just touching lips was not enough, so she pivoted. Both her hands took hold of Sallie Lee's shirt before she pulled it up and turned her attention to her lover's already erect nipples. She nipped and licked until Sallie Lee dragged her hand up Janet's body.

Sallie Lee braced her hands on the chest of drawers behind her. Janet undid the buttons on her slacks and eased them off her lover's hips. She knelt between Sallie Lee's legs and leaned into the dark thatch of hair, breathing deeply. She stroked a couple of fingers into the dew that glistened on the puffy labia and tentatively opened her lover up to her gaze. First kissing her lover on her inner thigh, Janet then focused her attention to the tiny nub.

"We're going to be late."

"Do you really want me to stop?"

Sallie Lee's breath caught. "Don't you dare."

"Don't worry."

Janet looked across the table to find Sallie Lee watching her. She smiled across the white linen tablecloth and blushed at being caught remembering why they were almost late for their reservation. She broke off a piece of bread and raised it to her mouth. Her face warmed, as she smelled Sallie Lee's scent on her fingers.

"What are you thinking?"

Blushing, Janet shook her head quickly.

"Come on. Tell me."

"I was remembering what we did before we came here."

"I think that blush means something else."

"I, uh, haven't washed my hands yet."

"Really?" Sallie Lee smiled.

Janet whispered, "I can smell you on my fingers."

"As a HACCP trainer, I am appalled by that news."

"HACCP? Sounds like you have hicups."

"It means hazard analysis and critical control point. It is how you can keep pathogens like salmonella, E. coli and listeria out of the food chain. If you can identify the points where danger exists you can set up procedures to keep everyone safe."

"Yeah. We had something like that in the kitchen in prison."

"What did they emphasize?"

"Keeping everything clean. Separate raw and cooked foods. Heating things hot enough to kill bacteria and cooling the leftovers down fast enough after the meal."

"So, I wonder what I should do to you to punish you for forgetting the first rule?"

"Punish?"

"Yes. I'll think of something while you go to the restroom."

"I'm not sure I like the sound of that."

"Believe me that you'll enjoy what I have in mind."

Janet made a face. "Really? Punishment?"

"Trust me, darling. I won't do anything that you don't want." Sallie Lee stroked her hand. "Please?"

"You're not going to hurt me?"

"No. Of course not, I just want to play with you some more."

"We're playing?"

"Yes. Do you want to try?" At Janet's nod, she continued, "Good. Now, you go to the bathroom and wash your hands properly. When you come back, I want you to do what I say."

Slightly confused by the turn of events, Janet pushed her chair back and stood up. "All right."

Sallie Lee grinned at her. "Hurry back." She enjoyed the vision of her lover as she moved around the tables on her way to the bathroom. The green slacks fit her trim figure very well and Sallie Lee thought back to the soft skin under them.

Returning to the table, Janet nervously fidgeted with her napkin. "So, what is going to happen now?"

"Well, I think that we have two situations that need to be addressed." She ticked off on her fingers. "One, you have refused to tell me what Della told you. Two, you failed to follow proper food handling procedures. What do you have to say for yourself?"

"Della didn't tell me much." Janet fiddled with her silverware and bread plate. "Just date stuff, what to wear, how to flirt." She squirmed at the end of the sentence.

Sallie Lee smiled. "Okay. I will let that one go. We still need to discuss cleanliness."

"It was you," Janet whispered.

"Excuse me?"

"On my hands. It was you."

"And that makes it okay?"

"I don't know. I guess not."

"No, it doesn't." Sallie Lee leaned back to allow the server to put a salad before her. She lifted her salad fork up and stabbed into the romaine. She slowly licked the dressing from the lettuce leaf before popping it into her mouth. She pulled the fork out of her mouth and quirked an eyebrow at Janet.

Janet's stomach dropped as she was pinned by her lover's gaze. She took a quick swallow from her water glass to wet her suddenly dry mouth.

"Now, what are you thinking?"

"I can't say it here."

"You want it to happen?"

"Yeah."

"Then you need to start talking." Sallie Lee grinned as she remembered what the two them enjoyed doing before they left home. "It's too bad that we were running late earlier. You just said you want me. What do you want exactly?"

Janet glanced around the restaurant. She began to speak in a low voice. "I want to feel your skin on mine. I want to be naked with you. I want to feel the different textures of your body with my fingertips. I want to feel the heft of your breasts on my palms. I want the sensation of your slickness against my thigh.

"I am sorry that I had to wash my hands. I loved the smell of you on my fingers. I want to paint your body with your juices and then lick every last drop off."

Taking a ragged breath, she continued, "When I woke up this morning, I was sore between my legs. All day, I have been missing the feeling of fullness I had from your finger penetrating me. I want you inside me again.

"I see the desire in your eyes and it makes me feel feverish. Everywhere you touched me last night feels like it is on fire. I can't sit still. I can hardly concentrate on anything else; I want you so badly.

"I am wet just thinking of what we have done before and in anticipation of doing it again."

"Wow. You are better at this than I ever imagined." Sallie Lee fanned herself with her hand. "I'm very proud of you and incredibly turned on." Sallie Lee put her credit card on the edge of the table and peered around the dining room for their server. "Let me pay this bill. After what I've just heard, I can hardly wait to get you home."

As Janet looked around, she felt as if the entire restaurant could smell her desire. She wondered if she would make it home before she exploded. "I'm glad we're going." She dropped her eyes to her untouched plate. "I seem to have lost my appetite for food."

"Don't worry. We'll have them put it in a doggie bag as I'm sure you're going to be hungry after I finish with you."

Janet whimpered. "Please, Lee."

"Don't worry, love. I'm going to take care of you."

CHAPTER TWENTY-TWO

"Thursday night is softball night," Sallie Lee announced as she pulled out of the driveway and headed to the restaurant. The skies were gray that morning, but the meteorologists were predicting that the haze would burn off by midafternoon. "I generally head over right after work. Is that okay with you?"

Janet regarded her steadily. "That sounds fine. Why haven't you been going the other Thursdays?"

"We had a couple of byes the week before and I was a little distracted last week." Sallie Lee reached over and squeezed her leg. "You had just come back into my life and I didn't want to miss a minute of it."

Janet cleared her throat and said, "I am a little concerned about the people."

"What do you mean?"

"I'm not real comfortable in crowds."

Sallie Lee nodded seriously. "I see. Do you want to stay at home?"

"I want to be with you."

"All right." She drummed her fingers on the wheel. "How about this? I'll leave you my car keys. If it gets to be too much, you got a place you can go to take a break." She tucked a strand of hair behind Janet's ear. "Will that work?"

"Thank you. I'm sorry to be so…" Her voice trailed off.

"Don't you worry your pretty little head about it." Sallie Lee fumbled with her key as another question occurred to her. "Do you have problems with the numbers of people in here?"

"Sometimes. I wonder what people know about me or what they think about what happened. It's easier knowing that I can stay back here and I don't have to go out front."

"I need you to let me know if it gets to be too much for you to handle." She handed over an apron but did not let go until Janet's eyes lifted to meet hers. "I need to trust that you'll tell me when you have a problem."

"Yeah. Okay."

"Not exactly a ringing endorsement but I will accept it for the moment. Now, let's go to work."

In no time at all, the workday was over and Janet was mopping down the floor while Della wiped down the tables and Sallie Lee ran the last of the dishes through the dishwasher.

They were quiet on the quick trip to the city limits. The Raphael Semmes Center was part of new development on the eastern outskirts. The multisports complex included a softball field and lighted tennis and basketball courts. It was a hive of activity this evening, with children and adults practicing, playing and waiting their turn.

When they got to the bleachers most of Sallie Lee's team was already hanging around, putting on their cleats, stretching, talking and laughing. They were waiting for the game ahead of theirs to finish and everyone was catching up on the happenings of each other's lives.

Janet sat by herself but she was rarely alone. Sallie Lee's team, the Playmakers, had heard about the new woman in her life and everyone wanted to have a chance to get to know Janet better. While they all knew that Sallie Lee was a lesbian, this was their first opportunity to study her choice of partner. They also delighted in the chance to tease the new lovers.

There were so many names and faces that Janet's head was spinning when the team finally headed onto the field to warm up. She could hear them continuing to laugh and banter as they took the field for the first inning.

Della arrived with her brood and introduced Janet to her husband and children. Daryl asked her if she remembered him from high school. She admitted that she did not and smiled when he did not seem to be bothered by it.

"Yeah, I didn't remember many underclassmen when I was a senior either." He looked at her. "I didn't know Jonathan at all except that he was a football god. Us junior varsity players idolized the guys on the field. We envied how they could get the girls." He hurried on after he saw her tense up. "It pisses me off to think of him forcing himself you."

Janet scrutinized him and Daryl shrugged one shoulder. "Considering his position, he could have had anyone. Instead, he was so fucked he had to nearly kill you to get it up. He was just lucky you got him. A lot of the guys with sisters would have happily taken a rock upside his head themselves." He nodded a couple of times before he walked away to grab a beer with his teammates. Janet could only stare after him and was startled when Sallie Lee touched her leg.

"Are you okay?" Sallie Lee asked. "I saw you talking to Man Mountain over there. He didn't say anything to upset you, did he?"

Janet looked wonderingly at her. "No. He thinks I did the right thing by killing Jonathan for what he did to me."

Sallie Lee placed a warm hand on Janet's knee and shook it gently. "I've been telling you since forever that the boy was pond scum."

"Yeah, but you are biased."

"Hybart! Get your butt back over here," Ida shouted. "Get into the on deck circle. You're batting next."

"Isn't this exciting? Only five more outs and they'll have

their first win of the season." Della dropped onto the seat beside Janet.

"Yeah. It's pretty cool."

"You could show a little more enthusiasm."

"I had forgotten how seriously people take their recreational sports."

"Don't let Lee or Daryl hear you speaking such blasphemy."

"I won't."

They watched Sallie Lee swagger up to the plate. Her confidence was really high after her last at bat several innings ago. She slapped the ball down in a bunt and hustled down the baseline beating the throw. She stood on the bag and pulled off her glove, shoving it deep into her back pocket. She gave a high five to the player standing in as the first base coach and tipped her hat to the stands.

When all was said and done and the inning was over, the Playmakers lost by one run. Grumbling good naturedly, they congratulated the other team before heading to the bleachers to eat and continue their conversations. The next game was almost over before Janet and Sallie Lee headed home.

CHAPTER TWENTY-THREE

The two women were in the living room, sitting at opposite ends of the couch with their legs touching as they read. After a long, hot day in the restaurant, they were enjoying the quiet companionship of their books, each other and the air conditioning. When the doorbell rang, they glanced at each other in surprise.

"Tammy," Sallie Lee exclaimed as she opened the door to a well-dressed contemporary of her parents. The cut of the charcoal dress did a lot to minimize her very full hips while her silver hair gave her a deceptively youthful appearance. "What brings you out here this late?" Sallie Lee asked as she ushered the other woman into the house.

"I need to talk to you." Stepping into the house with her color coordinating Marc Jacobs handbag dangling from one hand,

Tammy tried to smile. "I think I should speak to you both."

Concern evident on her face, Sallie Lee directed them all to the kitchen. "It is the best place to talk. Can I get you anything to drink?"

"No, thanks." The older woman sat heavily on one of the chairs and ran her fingers through her carefully styled hairdo. "I came here directly from the meeting."

Sallie Lee looked over at Janet. "Tammy serves on the county board of commissioners."

"I took over the seat after my husband died." She sighed. "Frank was in high hover tonight. His pet issue for the evening was the fact that there are felons in our midst."

Without even looking at her, Sallie Lee reached over and took Janet's hand. "Oh?"

"Yeah. He was most upset that we are sinking into the depths of depravity and endangering the welfare of our children."

"Inbred, needle dick bug fucker." Both Janet and Tammy looked at her in shock. Sallie Lee scrubbed her hand over her face.

"Name calling doesn't exactly help."

"Sorry, he just pisses me off. Are you sure who he was talking about?"

"Not dead sure, no." Tammy drummed her fingers on the table. "However, he mentioned Jezebel and the Semmes Sports Center. Everyone knows there were games the night before last and you both were there. I'm not the only one making the connection."

"I wonder who told him?" Sallie Lee mused. "He wouldn't be caught dead doing something as wholesome as exercise."

"Uh," Janet started to say.

"What, honey?"

"Who is Frank and why does he care?"

"Frank Yarborough is a weaselly little man who took his father's seat about five years ago. Before that he had a small congregation of Pentecostals until they caught onto his flimflam routine."

"What's his deal?"

Tammy answered, "He has appointed himself the moral

center of the board. He only speaks up to rattle his saber or to warn over the rising tide of corruption facing this town."

"His wife left him because he couldn't stay riled up long enough to finish her off."

"That isn't helpful," Tammy said severely. "Even if it is true." She looked at Janet. "Sallie Lee has been a target of his before."

"I've got to get out of here."

Both Tammy and Sallie Lee looked at Janet in surprise. She stood up and backed herself away from the table.

"Oh, no you don't." Sallie Lee got up to comfort her. "He can't do anything to you."

"Actually, he can."

The two women focused on the still sitting commissioner.

"Look, he claims that you didn't register with the sheriff's office when you settled in town." She questioned Janet. "Is that true?"

"I didn't know that I needed to. I'm not on parole, I served the full sentence."

"Alabama law requires all felons to register with the local authority." Tammy rapped her knuckles on the table. "Easily solved. All you need to do is go to the sheriff's office in the morning and register. Everything will blow over."

"It won't ever be over." Janet slid down the counter until she was sitting on the floor with her back against the cabinet doors. "I never should have come back."

Sallie Lee knelt down beside her. "Don't ever say that. The best thing that ever happened to me was you coming back into my life." She raised Janet's head and kissed her nose. "We will get this whole mess straightened out. You've served your time. No one can touch you now." The two women held gazes.

The ring of the timer came as a surprise and Tammy found herself pulling the cookie sheet out of the oven and moving the warm cookies onto racks. She watched Sallie Lee comfort the younger woman and smiled at the simple intimacy of the scene. "I'll leave you two alone," she finally said.

Sallie Lee turned to her. "Thank you for coming by and telling us. Want to take some cookies home?"

Tammy was sent home with a small baggie of cookies and Sallie Lee got Janet to sit down at the table again. She poured them both a glass of milk and set a plate of still warm cookies between them.

"Janet, honey, sometimes you amaze me."

Curious, Janet looked up at her. "What do you mean? I'm a basket case."

"Well, you are so very strong. You survived a horrible experience in the woods. You endured fifteen years in prison. You overcame your fears enough to love me." She paused. "You do love me, right?"

"Like I've never loved anything else in my life."

Sallie Lee smiled. "Glad to hear it." She placed a hand on Janet's leg. "I am amazed at all you have had to go through and that you are still standing."

"I'm not standing too well right now."

"That's just because you've eaten nearly a whole plate of cookies." With a serious expression, Sallie Lee continued, "Janet, I'm really surprised sometimes at how quick you are to forget all you've managed to accomplish."

"It isn't that much."

"Yes," she said with quiet emphasis. "Trust me. It is."

"I don't feel like I've done anything."

"How many people got their GED and BA in your cellblock?"

"Not many."

"How many of the folks who were released showed up back inside because they couldn't find legitimate work outside?"

"A lot."

"With all the trauma you've gone through, you're in remarkable shape." Sallie Lee used her thumb to wipe a bit of cookie crumbs off Janet's cheek. "I like the shape you're in." She brought her thumb to her mouth and sucked off the chocolate as Janet watched her every move.

"I think I missed some," she said softly as she leaned forward to lightly lick the same spot that her thumb had rubbed. Janet shivered and her eyes closed as their lips touched. "Umm. I need to remember how nice it is to taste chocolate off someone else's lips."

Janet pulled back slightly. "You need to know this for someone else?" she questioned with mock ferocity.

"I'm just going to file it for further reference." She reached up to bring Janet's head back toward her. "I won't act on it with anyone else but you."

"You better not." Janet found it hard to pretend to be angry when all she wanted to do was push the other woman down on the table and taste her. She smiled at the thought of Sallie Lee lying naked on the table.

"What are you smirking at?" Sallie Lee asked her lover after she felt the lips she was kissing curve into a smile.

"I'm thinking about where I want to taste chocolate off of you."

Sallie Lee regarded her silently for a moment. "Take me," she said simply.

When she saw the look of trust on her lover's face, Janet straightened her shoulders. "Let me take your clothes off." Janet said.

Moments later, Janet stepped back for a second and just gazed at the body she had revealed. Sallie Lee blushed as she saw the other woman staring at her. "What?" she asked.

"You are so beautiful," Janet replied. "I can't take my eyes off of you."

"I feel beautiful when you look at me like that."

Janet stepped forward and ran her palms over the length of Sallie Lee's back. "Your skin is so soft," she whispered into one ear before taking it into her mouth.

"Oh, you know what that does to me," Sallie Lee breathed as her aroused nipples stiffened even further.

Janet nuzzled her head between Sallie Lee's legs. "I love the way you smell," she breathed in the musky fragrance. Closing her eyes, Janet brushed the calf with her cheek before she continued to kiss her way toward the moist folds. For a moment, she rested her forehead on the damp curls and tried to steady her breathing. She was finding it hard to move slowly, all she wanted to do was to dive into Sallie Lee.

"Please." Sallie Lee's voice was throaty. "If you take too much longer, I'll explode."

Laughing, Janet said, "I can't have you do that without me." With a final glance into the dark eyes, Janet leaned her head down and placed the first kiss on Sallie Lee's mound. Slowly she used her tongue and lips to part the hair that was hiding her prize. The hard bud of Sallie Lee's clit was peaking out of its hood and Janet was gentle, moving her tongue alongside the labia before flattening it to press the length against the waiting spot.

"Oh, Janet," Sallie Lee moaned. "That feels so good."

Janet smiled as she moved her tongue to press its length into Sallie Lee's vagina. She drove it deep several times before she drew back to lavish attention on Sallie Lee's clit. She found a rhythm and brought Sallie Lee to the edge before she lifted her head and sucked on the arterial vein on her inner thighs. She was amazed at the powerful beat beneath her lips.

"Oh," Sallie Lee cried as she felt the warm pressure. Janet sucked the entire labia into her mouth, while continuing to tap her lover's clitoris with her tongue. The combination pulled even more blood from Sallie Lee's head and she arched her back.

Janet released the labia and concentrated on her clit. She stiffened her tongue and made a few short fast licks before suddenly flattening her tongue for a long movement. She vibrated her tongue quickly before repeating it all again.

Sallie Lee reached up to squeeze and fondle her own breasts as Janet continued to stroke her with her tongue. Her breathing was rapid. Janet didn't miss a beat as she brought her arms up to hold her lover's body against her mouth.

With a cry, Sallie Lee reached climax. Her upper body arched off the table and she tried to roll over onto her side. Janet stood up and pulled her limp form onto the floor and into her lap. She wrapped her arms around the still shuddering body and crooned softly to her.

CHAPTER TWENTY-FOUR

The next day dawned with a foreboding overcast sky and more than just the promise of rain. Janet was moving very slowly and Sallie Lee was trying hard not to lose her patience. She watched as her lover washed, rinsed and dried each individual dish they used for breakfast before she cracked.

"Enough, already. Let's just go and get this over with."

Janet looked up, her eyes shadowed. "I keep thinking about having to go back."

"You paid your debt. They can't do anything to you."

"They might find some other reason to hold me."

"That is not going to happen."

"How do you know?"

"Because I won't let you get railroaded into serving a sentence you don't deserve."

"How do you know I didn't deserve the last one?"

"Janet, I believe you defended yourself. You had every right to use force to save yourself."

"I couldn't sleep last night, thinking about what else could go wrong."

Sallie Lee stepped over to her and hugged her close. "Worrying about what might be can keep you from what is. Why don't we go in and find out?"

"I'm so scared," she mumbled into the comforting shoulder.

Sallie Lee released her and placed a quick kiss on the side of her mouth. "I don't blame you. I'll be with you all the way."

The two of them drove downtown to the sheriff's office.

Bill Warren had recently won re-election to the head law enforcement job. There were still a number of good ole boys in the county that opposed having a black man in charge of keeping the peace, but Bill's attention to detail had resulted in the closure of a number of open cases. Being a hero of the University of Alabama football team and a Heisman Trophy contender also helped him do his job. His large size and even temper seemed to manage to calm the most unreasonable drunk or unruly crowd.

"Good morning, ladies."

Janet jumped up at the rumbling sound of his deep voice. Slower to rise, Sallie Lee stuck out her hand. "Hello, Sheriff. This is my friend, Janet Bouton. We would like a few minutes of your time."

"Not a problem. Follow me." He directed them back into his office and turned sideways to get his broad shoulders through the doorway. His office walls were covered with pictures of him with many celebrities and politicians. Sitting down behind his desk, he waved them to seats on the couch beside it. "I didn't see you at the meeting last night."

"No, we had a visitor stop by afterward."

"Ah. Well, you know you've saved me a trip to your diner?"

"You can still come by afterward," Sallie Lee replied tartly.

"Yes, but now I will not be able to write the meal off as a legitimate expense." He gazed speculatively at Janet. "Young lady, did you know you're required to register with law enforcement when you come to a new location?"

"No, sir." Janet sat forward, making the leather sofa creak. "I just took the allowance and the bus ticket and walked out the gate."

He pursed his lips. "Well, they're supposed to give you a lecture or two on reentering society before just letting you go." He picked up a pencil and pulled out a form from the file cabinet beside his desk. "Where are you living now?"

Janet looked at Sallie Lee, who supplied her address.

"That is your home?" At her nod, he continued, "Where are you working?"

"At the diner."

"Are you responsible for the sudden increase in my deputies' pants sizes?"

"I do cook some of the time."

"She does most of the desserts and breads."

"I've been hearing nothing but good things about your place since I came to town."

"Thank you, Sheriff."

"Do you plan to stay in the area on a permanent basis?" he asked Janet.

Her eyes dropped to examine the geometric pattern of the green and ivory kilim rug on the floor. "I don't know. I didn't plan to stay here as long as I have."

"I see." In silence he filled out the rest of the form. "Well, you have a residence and a visible means of support. I'll have to check with the Department of Corrections to see if there were any conditions to your release, but I think that may be all I need."

"Really?"

"Yeah. I usually don't hold with interference from the council but I do need to check this out. You may want to stay out of the park until I get back in touch with you."

"We don't have another game until the Thursday after next."

"That should be plenty of time. I wasn't here when you came

through last, so I don't know all the particulars. You just go on as you were and I'll find you if there is a problem."

Janet nodded and wiped her damp hands on her pants.

That night, Della took his order to the kitchen. "Hey, one good thing from your trip to see The Man."

Glancing up, Janet frowned. "What?"

"The sheriff has come for dinner."

"What does he want?"

"Chicken for four, cold on wheels."

"Anything else?"

"No."

Sallie Lee shook her head. "Well, it's a start. We'll bide our time. He's going to crack someday."

Janet moved easily around the crowded kitchen and quickly filled a box with the chicken. "Did you offer him pie?"

"Yes, but he is a man of steel."

Sallie Lee picked up the box and carried it out front. "Here you go, Sheriff."

"I'm glad I caught you. Can the two of you come over tomorrow?"

"Sure. What's up?"

"I found some interesting stuff when I pulled the case file. Come by after lunch and I'll be ready to talk."

"All right. We'll be there. You have a good evening."

"I'll try. Good night, ladies," he called as he headed out the door.

"I wonder what he wants?"

"No use worrying about it now."

"I'm not supposed to worry? How is that even possible?"

"We just have to find something else to occupy our time and our minds." Sallie Lee grinned at her. "Are you willing to try?"

Janet blushed. "Della, can you finish locking up?"

"Go on and get out of here before you frighten the horses."

CHAPTER TWENTY-FIVE

"Thanks for coming in." Sheriff Warren stood as the two women entered his office. He indicated for them to sit down but he stood behind his desk looking uncomfortable. Today his uniform tie hung loose and there were dark puffy shadows under his eyes.

"Is there a problem?" Sallie Lee asked in concern, her hand automatically reaching out for Janet's.

"Well, yes and no."

"Would you care to explain?"

The sheriff dropped heavily into his chair and pushed an accordion folder across the desk. "This is for you."

"What is it?"

Clearing his throat, Sheriff Warren kept his eyes on the wall over their heads. "I spoke to the previous sheriff at length about what I found. The district attorney who prosecuted your case refuses to speak to me without his attorney present."

Janet looked confusedly at him. "I don't understand."

"I was curious and so I examined all the old files on your case. It took me most of yesterday just to sort through all the paperwork." He sighed. "There are a number of irregularities."

"Irregularities?" Sallie Lee asked, as she squeezed the hand of her lover.

"I put in this folder copies of documents that were never shared in the discovery process with Janet's original attorney. The information contained in them is exculpatory."

"What?"

"My predecessor didn't even bother to deny my accusation that he suppressed evidence." He nudged the folder closer to Janet. "I think you should have this reviewed by your own attorney."

"I'm sorry." Janet furrowed her brow. "I don't understand. What are you saying?"

"Ms. Bouton, I have to be honest with you. I cannot believe that charges were ever sustained against you."

"What?"

"My review of these materials casts serious doubts on your being responsible for Jonathan Garrett's death. You weren't the only one there that night. Furthermore, I think that you should consider pressing charges against those involved in your prosecution."

Janet stood abruptly. She muttered, "Excuse me," before she stumbled out the door.

Sallie Lee watched her leave. Turning to the sheriff, she bit out, "She served fifteen years."

"I know. It was a grave miscarriage of justice."

"What am I going to find in that folder?"

"Police and medical reports. Memos from lawyers."

"And what are we going to learn?"

"There were witnesses to her being dragged into the woods. A couple of reports tentatively identify the figures watching from the tree line when she was picked up on the highway. There's also a police report of the condition of the area around the body.

There were several sets of footprints." He paused. "They were not Janet's. You can see it all in there." He tapped the folder.

"Can I talk to you after we have a chance to go through this stuff?"

"I think you should retain an attorney. I'll be consulting the city attorney and I may not be able to speak with you as freely."

"What are you saying?"

He smoothed his hand down his tie and then over his eyes. With a heavy sigh, he raised sorrowful dark eyes to Sallie Lee. "The previous sheriff and the district attorney knowingly put an innocent person in jail. She did not get a fair trial then but she may be eligible for compensation for her false arrest and imprisonment. I don't think a jury would hesitate after being shown this evidence to do something for her pain and suffering."

"What do you think we should do?"

"I don't think you should let them get away with what they did to her."

Sallie Lee grabbed the folder and looked at the sheriff. "Thank you."

He bowed his head. "I apologize for my office."

Sallie Lee nodded distractedly and quickly walked outside. She found Janet being violently ill in the shrubbery outside of the station. Taking a moist towellette out of her purse, she tenderly wiped off Janet's face.

"Let me take you home."

"No. I don't want you to be late reopening. I can walk home."

"You can hardly stand upright."

"I'll be okay."

"No one would be okay after hearing what he said." Sallie Lee put an arm around her waist and led her across the square. "What are you feeling?"

"I don't know. I don't know what's real anymore. All those years..." Her voice trailed off. "I believed what they told me. I believed I killed him."

"Janet. I can't even conceive of what you are going through. But know that I am here for you."

She leaned her forehead onto Sallie Lee's shoulder. "I don't think that I could handle any of this without you."

"All right. Let's take this stuff to a lawyer instead of heading right back."

"It doesn't feel real to me yet. It's all happening so fast."

"Fast? Fifteen years is long enough to wait for justice."

"Who are we going to see?"

"One of the women I play against in softball practices criminal law. We'll try her first."

Janet silently followed as Sallie Lee changed direction and led the way over to the line of row houses next to the courthouse. Pushing open the door, Sallie Lee smiled at the receptionist.

Almost immediately after the receptionist had put down the receiver announcing the visitors, the connecting door opened. A trim young woman stepped into the foyer and smiled at her visitors. Well tanned and almost a foot taller than Janet, Emily had deep laugh lines and an easy smile. "Lee. It's good to see you. Are you here to sue your team for stranding you on base last week?"

"I only wish that would help them bat better. No, I have a miscarriage of justice case for you."

"Sounds like something I can sink my teeth into. Please, come on into my office, I'm free for a bit right now."

They followed her down the hallway. The dark paneled walls and severe portraits were a somber reminder of the longevity of this law firm. The room that they were led into faced the morning sun and was filled with blond wood and bright fabrics.

"Wow."

"Yeah. It's quite out of keeping with the tenor of the rest of the office, but all that dark wood gave me hives."

"And they let you do this?" Sallie Lee asked as they sat down in her comfortable chairs.

"They were pleased enough to do it. I bring in a lot of work." She flashed her very sharp, white teeth.

"Well, I've only heard good things about you."

"Thank you. So, what can I do for you?"

"Emily, this is my friend Janet Bouton. You might have seen her at the game on Thursday."

"How do you do?"

"Fine," Janet replied curtly.

"A while back, when she was still in high school, she was convicted of manslaughter and sent to prison. That folder contains information that the police and prosecutor suppressed that would have exonerated her. It was never shared with the defense."

Emily took the folder, her face solemn. "Where did you get this stuff?"

"Why?"

"I won't be involved in anything illegal."

"Sheriff Warren gave it to us. He was reviewing the case and found a file of information that had not been given to her original attorney." Sallie Lee drummed her fingers on the edge of the desk. "He offered us the rest of the materials too."

"I just bet the city attorney is going to be ecstatic when he hears about that." Opening the folder, Emily glanced through it. "Let me take a look at this and make a couple of calls. I'll call you after I have reviewed them."

"Great." Sallie Lee pulled out a business card. "Let us know if this is something you can handle or if we should go somewhere else. I've never been involved in this sort of thing before and you are the best lawyer I know."

"You'll turn my head with all that sweet talk. I should be able to get through this pretty quickly."

"The sooner, the better," Janet said softly.

"Yes, either call or come over to the restaurant."

"Thank you for stopping by. I'll be calling you." Emily leaned across her desk with her hand extended.

Janet stood up to shake her hand. On automatic pilot, she thanked the young attorney.

"Thank you." Sallie Lee led the way back into the sunshine.

They were quiet as they walked across the square to the diner. They entered through the front door and Sallie Lee took the back soon sign down. "Ready to get this show on the road?"

Janet nodded and tried to move by her to the kitchen.

"Hey."

"What?"

"Everything is going to be all right."

Meeting her eyes, Janet raised her hands in surrender. "When?"

"Honey, I'm with you on this. I'll help you see this through to the end. Whatever that may prove to be." She gazed critically at her lover. "You look like you could use a hug."

Janet raised grateful eyes. "Yeah. How did you know?"

"Babycakes, you can't hide such things from me." She opened her arms and Janet stepped into them. "You're safe here, honey."

Janet rubbed her nose against Sallie Lee's shirt. "Thanks."

"Anytime. You know you can ask for a hug anytime you need it, right?" She smiled at the shy shrug and released her. "Get into the kitchen, woman. We'll have customers soon."

It was late that afternoon when Emily called the restaurant. She spoke to Sallie Lee. "Look, I've done some preliminary work and I need to speak with you. Could you both come over at once?"

"You bet."

Sallie Lee relayed the news to Janet and again she closed the restaurant. Janet went into the bathroom to throw up.

Emily met them in the reception area and ushered them into the conference room and poked her head out into the reception area. "Clara, could you please get them something to drink while I collect my things?"

Janet paced the room like a caged animal while Sallie Lee watched her calmly, sipping her diet soda. Time seemed to pass with incredible slowness.

Finally, Emily came in and sat down at the table. "I've studied the papers you brought me from the sheriff's office. This stuff is dynamite."

"Does it mean I'm not guilty?"

"It means more than a reasonable doubt."

"So what can we do about it?"

Sallie Lee said, "Sheriff Warren said something about a motion to set aside judgment."

"Unfortunately, in this state you can only make that motion within thirty days of the verdict." She tapped her pen on the pad.

"Also, that's usually used when there's an error in the court's handling of the trial. My reading of this material shows that the error was entirely the prosecution's."

"Isn't there anything that can be done?"

"Oh, yes. There are a number of options left to us."

"But she'll have her name cleared, right?"

"I'm going to work very hard to do just that." Emily met both their gazes. "Look, any lawyer who gives you a guarantee about any decision of the court prior to the ruling is a liar and fool. Trust me that you don't want to be represented by someone like that."

Sallie Lee pointed at the piles of paper. "Haven't you looked at that stuff? The jury never got the whole story."

"I will not deny that there was a serious miscarriage of justice. I want to assure you that we have a good case for a judgment NOV."

"What does that mean?"

"It basically means notwithstanding the verdict. We are going to ask the court to reverse the jury's verdict because they would not have reasonably reached such a verdict if they had all the information."

"Then what?" Janet whispered.

"Then, it's like it never happened. The conviction is off your record."

"I'll be cleared."

"You'll be innocent."

"I always was." Janet shook her head in bewilderment. "I couldn't remember killing him because the truth is I really didn't."

Sallie Lee leaned over to her lover and squeezed her hand. She asked Emily, "Janet served fifteen years in jail. What can be done about that?"

"Well, I'll have to consult with a civil attorney, but I think you have a good case for a civil action against the city and against the particular individuals involved."

"What do you mean?"

"Damages. We can seek actual and punitive."

"You mean we'd sue?"

"Most definitely. Not only were you wrongly imprisoned and that can translate into a hefty pain and suffering settlement, but also your parents lost their business." She rubbed her hands together. "Did I read it right that you were planning for a medical career?" At Janet's nod, she continued, "Your lost wages alone will be a significant amount. There is the cost of your original legal fees, and, of course, interest on all that money. We are talking about a lot of damages." The lawyer came close to chortling with glee.

"Who is going to pay?"

"Well, the first thing to do is to investigate all the parties involved. I can't tell from my quick look how far up the food chain the culpability might extend. Once we do that, we can then figure out where the money is and go after it."

"Who do you think was involved?"

"There's the City of Pennington. There is also the sheriff's department and the district attorney. All of them are well covered by insurance and might be very open to a quick settlement. We might even have a case against your first lawyer for malpractice and, of course, there are the Garretts."

Janet interrupted her. "I don't want to be a part of a civil action against the Garretts."

"They are responsible for essentially offering a bribe."

"People offer rewards all the time for the arrest and conviction of criminals," Sallie Lee pointed out. "They couldn't have known that law enforcement and the judicial system would rig the system."

"Expectation or not, their efforts with the parole board had you serving the maximum sentence."

"Their son was dead and they wanted someone else to suffer."

"You certainly suffered."

"They gave the officials involved in this case a reward for an arrest and conviction. It's my bad luck that I fit the facts so easily." Janet pushed her chair back and stalked over to the window. "Everyone they put pressure on took an oath to uphold the public trust. They are the ones who should have to pay."

The lawyer looked challengingly at her. "Can you just forget that they came to your parole hearings? You can overlook that?"

"Did they know about the other information? Can we prove they knew I was innocent?"

"I doubt it very seriously."

"They were grieving."

"All right," the lawyer conceded. "Do you have any problems with the other people I named?" When Janet shook her head, she slapped her hands down on the table. "Good. This could take a while but I think we may be able to get you a pretty equitable settlement."

"I just want it over." Janet's voice cracked on the last word.

"I'll need you to make a commitment to this process. Once started, I want you to see it to the end."

"She'll go the distance. Just tell us what we have to do."

"Hold on. Not so fast. There are things that I have to consider before I take this case."

"Like what?"

"Well, we already know that there's evidence on your side. What's up in the air is whether you have the wherewithal to see it through."

"What do you mean?"

"First of all, there are my fees. I typically charge one-fifty an hour. The civil attorney works on a contingency basis so you won't have to worry about his fee until the case is resolved. Can you afford that?"

Janet shook her head. When Sallie Lee started to speak, she slashed her hand out. "No. You won't go into debt for me. My folks lost the diner the first go around. History is not going to repeat itself."

"You'll pay me back."

"How am I supposed to pay you? I already owe you for so much."

"Don't worry about it. Once you become a multimillionaire, you can pay me back."

"That brings me to my second point," Emily broke in. "There are going to be costs associated with gathering any additional evidence. We've got a lot of documents here. I just wonder how easy it will be to get anything else."

"What do you mean?"

"Attorneys for all the parties concerned are going to want to limit damages by limiting the free and easy access to police and prosecutor's records."

"But we have all this stuff."

"Sure, but we don't know the roadblocks that their attorneys are going to find."

"What are the steps?"

"Well, I need to file a complaint. Then there is discovery and then any motions or pretrial procedures. We then have them make a settlement or continue to trial. After the judgment is rendered and any post-trial motions or appeals are settled, we finish."

"We win?"

"Hopefully. We have to take into consideration that we may not get a favorable judgment. This is an old boy's network, which is why it's taken so many years and required the fresh blood of a new sheriff to bring this to light."

"What do we do now?"

"Let me go get a contract and have you sign it so we can get the ball rolling. I'll also need a retainer."

"How much?"

"I've already spent two hours on this and the initial motion filing will take at least another two. How about you pay for eight hours to begin with?"

"That is what? Twelve hundred?" Sallie Lee ignored the glare from Janet.

"Yes."

"Okay. I can do that."

Emily jumped up. "All right. Let me go get the paperwork."

Janet glowered mulishly, but Emily's quick return stopped her from arguing. She signed the papers and Sallie Lee wrote out a check for the retainer.

"Is there anything else?"

"No. The only question is how hard they'll work to find the real killer after all this time."

"What do we do next?"

"I should be in touch by Tuesday." Emily shook their hands.

Her eyes were lit with a crusader's ardor. "You were innocent, Janet. You were railroaded by corrupt officials and, together, we are going to clear your record and make them pay."

Somberly, the two women walked out of the lawyer's office into the sunlight. On the sidewalk Janet came to a halt.

"What is wrong?"

Janet breathed in deeply and slowly stretched. "For the first time in a long time I feel like I can stand up straight."

"What a weight to get off your shoulders."

"I feel like I've been born again." She smiled widely. "I'm *innocent.*"

"This calls for a celebration." Sallie Lee rubbed her hands together. "I know just the thing."

"Oh? Not another dinner out?"

"No. What we need is some banana pudding."

"That is celebration food?"

"I'm going to have to check your southern credentials. Banana pudding is a quintessential party food."

CHAPTER TWENTY-SIX

The last customer of the evening was handing over his credit card when the bell on the door jangled. Glancing up to let the newcomer know the restaurant was closing, Sallie Lee saw Sheriff Warren standing in the doorway.

He held his stiff brimmed hat in both hands. "Evening, everyone," he said when he realized that everyone in the place was looking at him.

"Is it a good evening, Sheriff?" Sallie Lee asked. Even though he had brought the mishandling of Janet's case to their attention, she could not help the feeling of resentment when she thought of law enforcement.

"There's no real way to go but up." Cracking the knuckles of his hands, he stood at the tableside looking down at her. "May I have a seat?"

"Of course. Do you want something to drink?"

"I wouldn't turn down a cup of coffee."

Della had been standing at the end of the counter and she reached for a mug before Sallie Lee could get up. She brought it and the pot of coffee over. "Shall I go get Janet?"

"Thank you," Sheriff Warren answered, taking a big sip of the scalding black brew. "Yes, please do. This concerns her."

Sallie Lee kept her eyes on the sheriff as he sucked down the entire cup. She noticed that the skin underneath his eyes was puffy and his shoulders seemed to droop with fatigue.

After Janet slid into the bench seat next to her, Sallie Lee said, "Well?"

"I came by to share some information. I sent off the forensic evidence from the case files to the lab in Montgomery for retesting."

"Really?" Sallie Lee asked. "You can do that after all this time?"

"Not all of it was any good anymore, but the currently available science is light years ahead of what we had back when the evidence was fresh. As it was, we got a hit back."

"A hit?"

"Yeah, under Alabama law, everyone who is arrested for a felony is compelled to give a DNA sample. Some of the blood matches that of two current guests of the Department of Corrections."

"The evidence you gave us should be enough to turn over her conviction. Why does it matter who did it?"

"Don't forget about the court of public opinion. Even though there was never anything but circumstantial evidence connecting her to the crime, she was arrested and charged."

"But she is innocent."

"You and I know that. Had the jury seen all the evidence, they would know it, but the reality is that they didn't. Folks like the Garretts and Frank Yarborough will continue to mutter that it was only a technicality that got her off."

"Technicality my ass. What they did was criminal."

Sheriff Warren smothered a laugh. "Be that as it may. The best thing is to have someone else found guilty."

"What about the guys whose blood you found? Can't you charge them?"

"There are a couple of problems with that." The sheriff cracked his knuckles. "Just the fact that someone else was convicted of the crime provides reasonable doubt for their guilt. Unless there is new evidence, even the worst defense lawyer could find enough wiggle room to get the jury to let them off."

"Don't these results count?"

"Unfortunately, the physical evidence only indicates that they were there that night. Unless Ms. Bouton got her memory back…"

Janet shook her head.

"Then we still don't have a live witness who can testify to what took place that terrible night."

"Maybe they'd confess."

"Those fellows aren't nice men. They've got a thick stack of prior arrests and are serving sentences greater than twenty-five years. There is no incentive we can offer for them to plead guilty to something that will only extend their time in prison."

"What about adding time concurrently? Can't they be offered that?"

"Considering the influence the Garrett family put on the judicial system with Ms. Bouton, do you really think the district attorney would agree to that?"

Sallie Lee shrugged. "Perhaps to have closure."

"No way," Janet scoffed. "She was furious with the lesser charge to me. I know she wanted the death penalty then."

Sallie Lee gently squeezed Janet's hand. "What can we do?" she asked.

"It is a long shot. I don't think these guys are monsters and Ms. Bouton might be able to convince them if she went up to Saint Clair and made a personal plea."

Janet pushed out of the booth and nearly tipped over a overturned chair on her way to the kitchen.

"Um…"

Sheriff Warren pointed at the still swinging door. "Go. Call me tomorrow and we can talk some more."

"Thanks." Sallie Lee placed her hand on his shoulder. "I

mean that. Thanks for not burying this and for running the tests. I know you didn't have to do that."

"If I wanted to live with myself, I did." Smiling wearily, he said, "Tell her I'm sorry."

"I'll lock up, Lee," Della added.

"Okay. Goodnight, y'all." Sallie Lee headed into the kitchen.

After a quick look around, she went through the back door and saw Janet nearly two blocks away and walking fast. Starting to jog, Sallie Lee was huffing and puffing when she caught up to her.

Dropping back to a walk she kept pace with Janet for few blocks as she got her breath back. She could see tears glistening on her cheeks.

As they were crossing the playground a couple of blocks from the Hybart home, Sallie Lee directed their steps over to the swing set. "I'm not ready to go home yet. Are you?"

Janet shook her head and sat down on one of the seats. They swung in silence for a while and it was fully dark when Janet slowly let her swing come to a stop. In the yellow light from the streetlights, she made patterns in the dirt with the toes of her shoes. Looking up into Sallie Lee's eyes, she said, "I can't go back inside."

"You'd be going as a visitor not a prisoner."

"I will never step through prison gates again."

"Even if it means you were free of this?"

"I am free of it." Janet smiled. "Wrongly convicted or not, I have served my time in hell."

"You wouldn't have had to serve a minute if those assholes had done their job properly."

"True enough and I'm sort of hoping that Emily finds a way to make them pay for that." Janet sighed. "What's also true is Jonathan is still dead. All the forensic evidence proves is that the clearing was pretty crowded that night."

"The medical record shows you were in no condition to harm anyone."

"But nobody knows for sure. Maybe I did kill him and then was beaten for it. Maybe someone else did it for what he did to me. I don't know and, frankly, don't care."

"Those guys might have information to completely clear your name."

"And they might just make it worse." Janet smiled weakly. "What happens if the lawyers here decide to bring the case back to trial? Even if I'm no longer the primary suspect, you know that a defense attorney is going to want to put me on the stand. Heck, they might even subpoena Julia Ann. How do you think she'll feel about that?"

Sallie Lee felt a little queasy at that thought. "She doesn't need that."

"None of us do." Janet stood up. "I'm closer to peace than I have ever been, thanks to you."

"I didn't do anything special."

"Not true. You believed in me from the first time I stepped into your place. You opened your house to me when I needed a place to stay. You opened your heart to me, defended me to the sheriff and paid the retainer for a lawyer."

"Anyone could have done those things."

"But no one else did. They weren't going to do a favor for an ex-con. They looked into things because of who you are." Janet clicked her heels together three times. "I never thought I'd say this but there is no place like home. You're the one who made Pennington that for me again."

"I love you."

"And I love you." Janet stood up. "I don't care what anyone else in this town thinks about me. I only care what you think. If you want me to do what the sheriff suggests, I will."

Sallie Lee took Janet into her arms. "I think you're very brave and, even though I don't understand your reasoning, I accept it. I won't push you."

"Thank you."

"You ready to go home now?"

"Yeah. It's been a long day."

"Remember to set your alarm at least twenty minutes earlier."

"Why?"

"We walked away without my car so we'll be hoofing it tomorrow."

"Oh, right."

"I'll call the sheriff tomorrow and tell him we won't be traveling up to any correctional facilities. I'll also let Emily know about the tests."

"Thank you." Janet leaned over and kissed Sallie Lee's cheek. "Your trust means a lot."

CHAPTER TWENTY-SEVEN

The lobby of the brick courthouse was cool in contrast to the rising heat of the morning outside. The small, somberly dressed group walked in from the bright sunshine and there was a general fumbling from everyone as they removed their sunglasses.

Janet walked forward to stand before the bronze statue of justice. Her eyes teared up as she contemplated the stern, blindfolded face.

Sallie Lee touched her arm. "You going to be okay?"

She swallowed. "I hate this place."

"After today, you might have better memories." Della stepped closer to her. "Justice may be blind, but she isn't stupid."

"This probably won't be over today," Emily warned them. "The court will need to review our documents and could possibly send this case back to the district attorney for a retrial." She stared hard at Janet, who was too miserable to notice. Turning to Sallie Lee, she said, "You have to keep her in balance for this thing."

"She'll be fine."

"We should have come here before the case was called. It would have been better if we'd done a run-through before all this." The group was at the door to the courtroom. "No matter. Just keep her calm."

Sallie Lee reached out and took Janet's hand. "Don't worry. She can handle this."

"Stop talking about me like I'm not here."

"Sorry, love."

"I'll be okay."

"I know you will. I also know this is really hard." She swung Janet's hand back and forth. "We're here for you."

"Thanks." She tightened her grip as the small group entered the courtroom.

The tall ceilings added to the sense that they were under the power of laws. Along the front wall, behind the judge's bench, were the Alabama State Seal and flags for the United States and Alabama. There were several people already sitting in the public area.

Sallie Lee smiled at a reporter from the local paper as she followed Emily. The lawyer, trim in her dark suit, led them to the right-hand side and pointed to the first line of chairs behind the bar. "Everyone but Janet and I needs to wait here. Don't read anything. Judge Williams hates that."

She directed Janet to the large oak table and she began to lay out her materials. Besides the pad of legal paper, she had the case law book and a stack of documents for exhibits. She glanced up when one of the lawyers from the other table approached them.

The district attorney, Jack Waterman, was in a brown suit that was stretched tightly across his belly. His jet black hair was slicked back, showing off his wide forehead, pocked with acne scars.

"Ms. Myers. Ms. Bouton."

"Good morning, Jack. How are you?"

"I could be better."

"On such a beautiful day?"

"I would feel better if I didn't have to be here today."

"You know, the easiest way to avoid this would have been for you to return my phone calls."

"Frankly, I didn't think you'd be able to get her this far."

"I didn't know you knew my client."

"I don't know her personally, but I did call the warden up at Tutwiler and learned a little about her."

"She had a good record up there."

"Sure she did. She also failed to follow through on a couple of programs that would have gotten her out sooner."

"Considering that she shouldn't have been in there in the first place, I hardly think her not taking advantage of the early release program should be counted as a strike against her."

He shrugged. "Be that as it may. Before we take too much of the court's time, I'd like to get a feel of what it would take to settle this thing."

"Reverse the original guilty verdict, stipulate that you will not seek a new trial and provide appropriate damages."

"No one in my office wants to see this case retried. We will agree to join your petition to the court to set aside the trial verdict."

"And damages?"

"What are we talking about?"

"You have the papers with my breakdown."

"Let's pretend I can't remember."

"Ten million."

"Let's pretend you said five point five."

Emily put her hand on Janet's shoulder. "Give me a moment to speak with my client."

When Jack stepped back across the aisle, she dropped into the seat. "Well? He is agreeing to all our demands. He is even five hundred thousand over what we agreed was our minimum settlement amount."

Janet's voice was hoarse. "What do you think?"

"It's a good deal."

"If we do agree, this is it, right? We're done."

"Correct. All that would be left is signing the paperwork and endorsing the payment plan."

Looking over her shoulder and scanning the faces of her friends, Janet saw only support. She nodded. "Let's do it."

Emily beckoned the opposing counsel over. "I want the paperwork on my desk by three o'clock."

"It has been a pleasure doing business with you, Ms. Myers." He held out a hand to Janet. "Ms. Bouton, I would like to apologize for the actions of my office."

Tentatively, she quickly squeezed and released his hand. She stood up and pushed through the barrier. Flinging herself into Sallie Lee's arms, she clung desperately to her lover.

Sallie Lee looked over her shoulder. "It's over?" she asked the lawyer.

Nodding at the small group, Emily stuffed her papers into her briefcase. "Yes."

"That was a lot faster than I expected."

"They didn't want the publicity. I mean, if the police and prosecution behaved so poorly in this case, they probably did it in others. Every verdict of the past fifteen years could be in jeopardy."

"That's almost too scary to think about."

"So think about what you're going to do with five point five million, minus expenses and attorney's fees."

"I never expected that much money. I thought you were crazy to ask for ten."

"Crazy like a fox," Sallie Lee said with a laugh. "Thank you so much, Emily."

"Just doing my part for truth, justice and the American way."

"Great. I want to invite you all back to our place for a celebration."

"We're not opening the restaurant?"

"No, we've got more important things to do," Sallie Lee said.

Janet stayed wrapped in Sallie Lee's arms as the older woman coordinated getting everyone into cars and over to her family's house.

The group piled into their own cars. Everyone was laughing in hysterical relief as they joined Janet and Sallie Lee in the kitchen.

"What we need is something to drink." Sallie Lee opened the freezer and pulled out some lime juice that she had frozen at the beginning of the season.

The festive group hung around the kitchen, talking and laughing the afternoon hours away. Janet could not keep the smile off her face as these, until recently strangers, congratulated her on her victory and welcomed her into their fold.

It was full dark by the time Sallie Lee and Janet were alone in the house. She took one look at her tired and slightly buzzed lover and smiled. "Why don't you head upstairs and I'll run you a bath?"

"I'll just take a shower."

Sallie Lee picked up several empty glasses. "Go on up." She bumped her hip against Janet's. "I'll meet you in the master bath." She quickly loaded the top rack of the dishwasher and set it on rinse and hold. Switching off the lights, she checked the locks on the doors before she climbed up the stairs.

Humming to herself, Sallie Lee chose the bottle of rosemary scented herbal bath oil from the crowded shelf of bath products. She poured a capful of the red liquid under the stream of warm water and took a deep breath of the heady steam.

She turned to see Janet standing in the doorway. Her lover's dark head was drooping in exhaustion, her tired eyes staring at the pattern in the tiles.

Clucking her tongue, Sallie Lee pulled Janet unresisting toward the Jacuzzi tub. Wordlessly she undressed her before she stripped out of her own clothes. "Go on, get in."

"I don't need a bath."

"You'll feel better afterward, I promise." Moving carefully so as not to displace too much water onto the floor, Sallie Lee lowered herself down behind her.

"Lean back against me," she encouraged with steady pressure on the tight shoulders. Janet tentatively slid down and nestled her head against Sallie Lee's throat.

"Does that feel good?" She murmured as she took an

exfoliating puff and the black glycerin Magno soap into her hands. Sallie Lee worked up a rich lather and slowly moved the washcloth over Janet's neck and shoulders. Almost imperceptibly, she felt the stressed woman relax against her. Steadily, she trailed the soapy material across the skin of her lover, gradually moving the cleaning cloth down her upper arms and chest.

Picking up one of her lover's arms, Sallie Lee washed her hand and forearm. When Janet tried to take the sponge, she held it out of reach. "Just take it easy."

Janet wiggled her body against her lover. "Can't I help?"

"Close your eyes and relax," Sallie Lee whispered. "No worries, love. You don't have to do anything. Just lie here and feel my hands on you."

"This is making me very sleepy," Janet mumbled. She lazily turned her head and nuzzled Sallie Lee's jaw. "Is that your plan?"

"One of many." Sallie Lee smiled and turned her head to kiss her lover. She relished the feeling of Janet's soft skin on hers, the precious weight of the body on top of her.

"You have more than one?"

Sallie Lee moved the washcloth down to just above the surface of the water and over Janet's hardening nipples. The younger woman gasped and arched, pressed up into the erotic touch.

"I do have an ulterior motive, darling. You've had a really stressful time and I want to take care of you."

"I want to touch you." Janet tried to shift on her side.

Sallie Lee held her in place. "Whoa. We'll get to that later." She tenderly bit the ear closest to her mouth. "Can you wait while I take care of some unfinished business?"

"I'm not good at waiting."

"Yes, you are very impatient. Remember, though, good things come to those who wait."

"If you keep teasing me like that, I'll come without waiting."

"Then, open for me, baby." Sallie Lee hooked her heels around the inside of Janet's ankles and pulled her legs apart. "Just lean back and let me have my wicked way with you."

Janet's breathing quickened as the warm water lapped against her private parts. "That feels good."

"That's it, sugar," Sallie Lee encouraged. "Spread out for me."

The younger woman slowly did as she was asked.

Sallie Lee tossed the puff to the side and slid her palm down Janet's rounded belly. She gently scratched a trail up the smooth skin of Janet's inner thighs causing the muscles to jump. Winding her fingers through the dark hair, she sought out Janet's swollen clit. "Your skin is so soft."

Exploring the supple folds of her lover's labia, Sallie Lee's touch brought another moan from her lover's throat. Involuntarily, Janet pulled her knees farther up.

"Good girl. Open up, let me in." Letting her other hand join the first, she gently pressed her middle and ring finger against the tight muscle of her lover's vulva.

"You need to relax. Trust me." Her lips only a breath away from Janet's ear, the caress of her lover's voice caused Janet to shiver. "Good girl. Doesn't this feel good?"

"Yes," Janet moaned. "I want…" Almost completely incoherent from the feelings rushing up from her toes, Janet rolled her head back and forth.

"Do you want me to stop?"

"No, please don't." Her hands clenched and released spasmodically.

Sallie Lee's voice was husky with desire. "This is driving you wild, isn't it?"

"It's so much."

"Tell me if it gets to be too much." Sallie Lee thrust gently. "Do you like being so exposed?"

"Yes."

"You're so close. I can feel your muscles trying to hold me inside."

"So close."

"You want to come so bad. I can give you that release." She toyed with the erect clit; just barely making contact while her other hand penetrated her.

"Lee," Janet whimpered. "Please."

"You don't have to beg, Janet. Not this time." Sallie Lee assured her. "Just let go. Please, come for me."

The simple plea and the intrusive, probing fingers sent her over the edge. Janet's body went rigid as she clenched her legs, pinning her lover's hands to her hot center. Continuing to undulate her fingers, Sallie Lee whispered, "Again."

Biting her lip, Janet struggled to calm her breathing as another orgasm rocked through her. "Oh, Lee."

Sallie Lee wrapped herself around the woman she loved and held on to her. "It's okay. I've got you. I'm right here."

CHAPTER TWENTY-EIGHT

Janet was lounging on the patio and watching Sallie Lee putter in the garden. The powder blue tank top she was wearing was darkening with sweat as she worked her way down each row, weeding and plucking ripe fruit and dead leaves off the still producing plants. She was jolted out of her reverie of the skintight athletic shorts stretched across her ass when she saw Sallie Lee glaring at her over the top of her sunglasses.

"You told me you weren't helping me because you needed to take a nap. Not because you wanted to sit up there and ogle me."

"Can I help it if I've just got a wonderful view?"

"If you're not going to get out here, you can get your lazy butt up and get me some iced tea. This is thirsty work."

"That I can do." Janet opened up the door and heard the phone ringing. "Hey, you've got a call."

"Can you take a message? My hands are filthy."

"Sure." Janet picked up the receiver. "Hybart residence."

"Who is this?"

"For whom did you call?"

"My sister."

Janet stilled. "Is this...Is this Julia Ann?"

"Yep. Knowing my sister, you're not the cleaning lady."

"You'd be surprised. I do everything these days but windows."

"Funny."

"Thanks. Lee is outside playing in the dirt. Do you want to hold on while she cleans up or do you want her to call you back?"

"How about I talk with you while I wait for her."

"Huh?" Janet looked bewilderedly at the phone before putting it back to her ear. "Why do you want to talk to me?"

"I owe you an apology."

"No, you don't. You don't have to mention it. Seriously, don't mention it. I'm going to put the phone down now."

"Don't trivialize this and don't hang up on me!" Julia Ann exclaimed. "Look, I realize this is as hard for you to hear as it is for me to say."

"You don't need to do this."

"Yes, I do. We both need this closure. I am very sorry that I abandoned you back then and never supported you like you needed."

Janet blinked rapidly to clear away the tears. "You were hurting, too."

"I was still wrong. I was an idiot to think it was all about me and how his murder and your injuries ruined my life." Her sigh was loud over the phone line. "It took me years of therapy to get my head out of my ass and, by then, I figured it was too late for me to do anything."

"It's okay."

"No, Janet, it's really not. Rectal-cranial inversion is a serious condition that affects more than just the victim." She paused. "That was a joke and you can laugh."

"Sorry. Um, ha, ha."

"Don't strain anything. After you went away and your parents passed, I should have said something or done something but I tried like hell to forget that part of my life ever existed."

"Did it help? Did forgetting it make things easier?" Janet asked. "It never really seemed to help me."

"That's just it. It didn't work for me either. On the contrary, it has influenced nearly everything I've done, including my career choices."

"Lee says you're a social worker."

"I work primarily with survivors of sexual assault."

"Oh." Janet scratched her head. "That must be hard."

"It was necessary. I've felt guilty for years—"

"What do you have to be guilty of?" Janet interrupted. "Did you know what he was going to do? Did you make those guys kill him or force those stupid lawyers to make up stuff so I could be sent away?"

Pacing around the room, Janet could feel her body tensing up as her voice rose. "Did you drive the truck that smashed my folks? Did you pay them to rape me in prison or write letters to the parole board to keep me there for so long? Did you do one damn thing to me?"

"Breathe, Janet. Have a seat in the chair by the phone and just breathe for a minute or two."

Janet closed her eyes and obeyed the order. Counting silently as she inhaled and exhaled, she finally muttered, "Sorry. I'm okay."

"I know you are. You also have every right to be angry."

"I don't know why you want me to be mad at you." Janet rubbed her stinging eyes with the back of her hand. "You were my friend."

"I failed you as a friend. I hope that someday you can forgive me."

"I miss our friendship." Janet picked at a loose thread on her shorts and slowly began unraveling the hem. "You know the court set aside that verdict, right?"

"Yeah, Lee sent an e-mail."

"The decision sort of cleans the slate for me. I'd be stupid not to do the same for everyone else."

"What are you saying?"

"I don't think you really did anything wrong but I pardon you."

"Thank you, Janet." Julia Ann loudly blew her nose. "I'm so glad you picked up the phone."

"Me too."

"You are also welcome to call me sometimes too. I might not be able to take sides against my sister but I can try to help you if you ever have issues you need to discuss."

"You think I have issues?"

"No one on the planet escapes without some scarring from life. You've had things rougher than most and the roller coaster of the past couple of months can't be helping things."

"I've done pretty well so far."

"You've done remarkably well but talking helps. Perhaps you should think about using some of that settlement money to pay for someone to listen to you."

"I don't like talking to strangers."

"Sometimes a stranger can give an objective perspective. Chatting with friends can be helpful, but they aren't trained and they aren't impartial when approaching your problems."

"A little bit of bias can't be bad."

"It is if it means you won't be completely honest, especially about things that are embarrassing or painful or private."

"In prison, they could use what you talked about against you."

"Because they were paid for by the prison. Independent professionals are bound by confidentiality. They can't blab your secrets to the world."

"You really think I should do this? And not just because this is what you do for a living?"

"Yes, Janet, I think it will help you come to terms with all you've been through. Even if you don't open up entirely, a good therapist can help give you tools to deal with the things that are causing you problems."

"Like what?"

"Like how to deal with flashbacks during sex."

Janet felt dizzy. "How do you know about that? I haven't told anybody."

"Nearly every sexual assault survivor experiences them. A therapist could help you understand what triggers you and how to ease the feelings of panic by giving you grounding exercises."

"Oh." Janet swallowed. "That could help."

"Definitely. I'm glad you're open to the possibility but don't do it just because I'm advocating for it. Unless you go because you want to get better, you won't get much out of it. It may also take a while for you to find someone you're comfortable opening up to."

"What about pills? Couldn't I take a prescription instead?"

"Medication alone is totally inadequate," Julia Ann replied. "You need to talk about what you survived."

"I'll think about it."

"Excellent. That's mainly what I wanted to speak to you about. I hope we're able to talk more in the future."

"I think I'd like that."

"Good. I'm very glad you've found your way back to Lee."

"You know about me and Lee?"

"I've known since high school when you used to sneak in her room and mess with her laundry."

Appalled, Janet whispered, "You haven't told her that, have you?"

"Of course not. That is a BFF secret that overrides sister privilege."

"BFF?"

"Best friends forever."

"Oh, I'd like that. I think I need more friends."

"I'd be honored to be yours again."

Janet sat there with the phone cradled in her arms. She glanced up when a shadow fell over her and quickly wiped her eyes. Opting for a casual tone, she asked, "Hey, Lee. Are you done outside?"

"No, I was wondering where you got to with my tea. Are you okay?"

"I'm getting there."

"Did you get a call that upset you?"

"Julia Ann called and we talked. We really talked." Janet put down the phone and stood up. "Can I get a hug?"

"I'm a little dirty."

"I don't care." Janet pulled Sallie Lee close.

"Was she mean to you?"

"No. She wanted me to forgive her and to be friends again. It's just so much at once. I need help holding it all together."

Sallie Lee's arms tightened until Janet squeaked. "Oof, not so much."

"Sorry! I'm just happy that you two are connecting."

"Aren't you afraid of the J-Birds uniting against you?"

"Not if you don't want to go back to sleeping in separate beds." Sallie Lee grinned. "You're both part of my family and I'm ecstatic that you're getting along again."

"Family?"

"You bet you are." Sallie Lee kissed her. "Family means more to me than DNA. Family is those people who love you, no matter what you do or who you are."

"I like that idea."

"We all have a family we were born in, but the best family members are those you choose."

"I choose you." Janet looked deep into Sallie Lee's eyes. "I love you."

"Why don't you show me?"

Janet laughed and stepped back out of her arms. "Because you're filthy."

"Join me for a shower first and I'll show you just how fun dirty can be." Sallie Lee grabbed Janet's hand and led the way upstairs.

CHAPTER TWENTY-NINE

It was five minutes before closing when the door to the restaurant opened. The clanging bell seemed to startle the white-haired woman and she hesitated in the doorway. Wearing a somber navy blue dress, she held her large purse in front of her like a shield. Letting the door fall closed behind her, she fixed her blue eyes on Della.

Della looked up from wiping tables and smiled at the older woman. "Hello. We are just about to lock up for the night. Is there something we can get you? You'll have to get it to go."

"I want to talk to her," she demanded.

"Talk to who?"

"Miss Bouton."

"You mean Janet?"

"Yes."

"All right. Let me check… Oh, Lee," Della interrupted herself as Sallie Lee stepped up front with the supply checklist in her hand. "She wants to see Janet."

Stopped dead still in the doorway, Sallie Lee did not move even after the swinging door hit her backside. "Mrs. Garrett. What do you want?"

"I want to talk to her."

"I don't think that is such a good idea."

"I don't really care what you think. This is between the two of us."

"Anything that is going to upset her, affects me." Sallie Lee tossed her clipboard down on the counter and crossed her arms. "Why are you here?"

"There are things that need to be said."

"You had plenty of chances."

"Not knowing what I know now." The older woman seemed to shrink somewhat. "Please."

It was that one word that decided it for her. "I'll go get her. But if she doesn't want to talk, you'll leave."

"I'll go after I've said my piece."

"No. You'll go without a problem if she wants you to go."

Once Mrs. Garrett nodded in agreement, Sallie Lee pushed the door open and saw Janet bent over, loading the dishwasher. She called, "Honey?" When Janet looked at her, she asked, "Could you come out here, please?"

Wiping her hands on her apron, Janet moved easily to Sallie Lee's side. The smile on her face died once she caught sight of the woman clutching her handbag to her chest. Instinctively, she tried to back up but Sallie Lee was behind her, blocking her path to the kitchen.

"She has something to say to you," Sallie Lee murmured in her ear.

"Janet Bouton."

Trembling, Janet did not answer. She could only stare at a vision from her nightmares. In front of her was the woman who had testified at her sentencing and at every parole hearing. Sallie Lee placed her hand on Janet's back, offering her silent support.

"I tried to contact you through your lawyer, but she told me you refuse to talk to me."

"I don't have anything to say."

"I do."

"There isn't anything I want to hear," Janet said desperately. She pressed back against Sallie Lee.

"I need to say it anyway." Taking a deep breath, Mrs. Garrett moved a step closer but halted when Janet flinched. "I want to apologize to you. I need to tell you how very sorry I am." When Janet opened her mouth, she raised her hand to forestall whatever Janet was trying to say. "I realize how inadequate those words are. Nothing I can do would repay you for the time you have lost. I beg you to forgive me."

"You just wanted justice. You acted out of love."

"Love doesn't seek revenge and that's what I did. I was blind with anger and hate. I couldn't let it go. I never believed that you couldn't remember what happened. I wanted you to rot in jail until you admitted what you did." She looked at the pale young woman across the room. "I don't deserve your forgiveness, but I am asking for it anyway."

Janet stood frozen in the doorway. She angrily dashed tears from her eyes. "Did you know?"

"Know what?"

"About the evidence that someone else was involved."

"No. I only knew what I heard at trial. We offered a reward, but that didn't give us any special information." Mrs. Garrett held out her hand. "Please believe me that I am as shocked as you."

"You didn't have to wonder every day for seventeen years if you really killed somebody."

"No, that must have been awful. But don't you see? I would never have sanctioned the hiding of evidence because I wanted the killer of my son brought to justice. Whoever did it is still out there."

Turning her head, Janet stared into Sallie Lee's loving eyes. She swallowed around the lump in her throat and nodded. "Okay."

"I beg your pardon?"

"I forgive you."

Mrs. Garrett looked slightly startled. "Thank you." She cleared her throat. "I have another request." When Janet only raised an eyebrow, she hurried to explain. "I would like to get a copy of the information your lawyer has."

"Why?"

"I'm not going to rest until his killer is behind bars."

"What if they already are?"

"I beg your pardon?"

"What if they are already in prison, serving time? Would you let it go then?"

Mrs. Garrett's pale eyes glittered. "What are you saying?"

"Sheriff Warren retested the DNA from the clearing. The guys who left it are in maximum security for the rest of their lives. Isn't that enough?"

"My son's killers must pay for what they did."

"It isn't going to bring him back."

"He deserves justice."

"Justice? He was no angel and your crusade isn't going to resolve anything. Let him rest in peace."

"There won't be any peace until someone is punished."

"Says someone who has never spent a night in prison. I don't want any part in this," Janet said, her voice laced with exhaustion. "But I won't stop you."

"Thank you. I appreciate it."

Without responding, Janet moved around Sallie Lee and headed back into the kitchen. Sallie Lee watched her disappear behind the door before turning back to their visitor. "Did you need anything else?"

"No. I'm so sorry."

"Yeah, I'm sorry for all the time she lost."

"At least she can make it up. My son will never have that chance." Mrs. Garrett nodded at the two women. "Good day."

Without a further word, she left the restaurant. Della and Sallie Lee stared through the window as she marched down the street.

"What a battle-ax."

"Yeah. I can see why the parole board listened to her, though."

"I'm going to take Janet home. Will you be all right by yourself?"

"Sure. Take care of her."

"I'll do my best."

Janet was quiet for the journey home. She only shook her head when Sallie Lee told her to go take a bath while she fixed something to eat.

"I'm not hungry."

"You might be later. Go on. You'll feel better after a good soak."

"I'll just shower and head to bed."

"The tub is better." Sallie Lee raised her hands in surrender at Janet's glare. "Don't mind me. Do what you like."

"Thank you."

"What?"

"Thank you. You've been great through all this."

"You're welcome. Thank you for letting me be there for you." She laughed. "Now that we have pledged our mutual admiration for one another, why don't you go upstairs?"

Some time later, Sallie Lee knocked softly on the bathroom door. Janet had been in the shower for a very a long time and she was concerned. There was no way that there was any hot water left. She pushed open the door and stepped into the room. Seeing Janet curled up in the floor of the stall, she moved quickly to her side.

"Janet, are you hurt?" Sallie Lee asked urgently as she shut off the water and knelt down beside her. When her lover did not say anything, she gently pulled the wet form against her. "Speak to me, baby."

Unable to talk, she clung to her lover as her body was racked with sobs. Unused to such violent sorrow, she fought against the release and it left her heaving and gasping for air. Slowly, as Sallie Lee rocked her, the weeping wound down.

Sallie Lee looked down and saw Janet staring up at her. "What?"

"I can't seem to stop crying."

"There's nothing wrong with that."

"I hate it."

"What exactly is so hateful? I kind of like it. I feel so free when I'm done."

"I'm doing it all the time and it hurts."

"What does?"

"My chest aches and my eyes are swollen. I can't breathe and I get a bad headache."

"That's because you have so many years of tears saved up. Catharsis can be painful when you start."

Janet's voice was soft. "I'm so confused."

"Maybe you should talk to someone."

"Lee…"

"Look, I know you don't want to hear about this but please listen. Your entire life has been turned upside down not once but multiple times. You were raped. You spent years thinking you had done something horrible in a truly frightening place. You now know you're innocent, but all you've been through takes a toll." Sallie Lee pulled a towel around the shivering woman.

"Even when it's over, it's not over."

"You can't be expected to deal with it alone. I'm here for you but I'm hardly qualified to give you all the help you need."

"I'm so tired."

"It's exhausting to feel."

"Then why should I?"

"Because it is also extremely exhilarating." Sallie Lee tugged on her lover's arm. "Let's get up and get into bed. I'm stiffening up here on the floor and you are freezing."

"I don't know if I can sleep."

"We can lay down and I can hold you."

Janet nodded and allowed herself to be dried off and led to the bed. She curled into Sallie Lee's arms. "I like this."

"You and me both." Sallie Lee ran her fingers through the wet hair. "You're going to have a rat's nest here in the morning."

"I didn't really do anything in there but cry. I still need to take a shower before work."

"Did you plan on breaking down in there? Is that why you didn't take a bath?"

"I didn't want to upset you."

"Give me some credit. You don't need to hide your emotions from me."

Janet yawned hugely, her jaws cracked. "Sorry."

"Go to sleep. We'll talk more tomorrow."

"Are you threatening me?"

"I'm promising you that if I ever leave you, it won't be because you feel something. You only upset me if you lie about what's happening."

"I didn't lie. I just don't want to be a burden."

"Let me hold you when you're hurting. A burden shared is a weight halved."

"Who said that?"

"I did. Pretty deep, huh?" Sallie Lee's arms tightened around her. "You're my lover and I want to be there for you on the highs and lows."

"I'm getting a little dizzy from all the ups and downs."

"And I'm not going anywhere."

"Good. I'm happy you're here with me."

"Glad to hear it. You make me pretty happy too." Sallie Lee kissed the dark hair. "Shall I sing you a lullaby?"

"You can sing?"

"Of course. I sang in the chorus all through school."

"That's right. You did everything."

"Not quite everything. At least I never had to stoop to working on the yearbook."

"Shut up. What are you going to sing?"

"Do you have a request?"

"How about 'Will the Circle be Unbroken?'"

"I can do gospel tunes." Sallie Lee closed her eyes and tried to remember the words. As she began to sing, her voice was unsure but it gained strength once she hit the first refrain of "Will the Circle be Unbroken."

She finished singing the song and gently turned Janet so that she could spoon behind her. Very softly, she whispered, "I love you," into the sleeping woman's ear. In short order, she soon joined her lover in dreams.

Lying restlessly in the bed, Janet tried not to disturb Sallie Lee. Finally, she turned over and looked at the illuminated dial of the clock on the nightstand. It was two thirty in the morning and she had never felt the darkness more keenly. Carefully, she climbed out from under Sallie Lee's arm and snagged her shirt off the floor before walking downstairs.

She took the business card that Ida had dropped off at the restaurant and ran her fingers over the embossed lettering. She sighed and walked over to the phone hanging on the wall.

Janet listened to the doctor's voice mail message asking her to wait for the tone. "Hello. My name is Janet Bouton. Ida referred me to you and I would like to make an appointment with you to talk. Um, to talk about my problems. I will try to call you again tomorrow, I mean later today. Let me give you my number…" When she hung up, she had to wipe her damp hands on her T-shirt.

She turned off the light and made her way back up the stairs to the bedroom.

For a long time, Janet stood beside the bed. There was enough light coming through the partially open window to illuminate her sleeping partner. She reflected over violating Sallie Lee's privacy like this. Watching someone sleep was an amazingly intimate act. But she could not help herself.

Sallie Lee was on her side with one arm holding the pillow to her chest and the other flung into the space on the bed that Janet usually occupied. The sheet was bunched at her feet and Janet gazed at the nude form before her.

As if she could feel the gaze, Sallie Lee's eyes fluttered open and her arm swept over the cold sheets. She sat halfway up before catching sight of her lover standing by the bed. She brushed her bangs out of her eyes while she reached toward Janet. "Are you okay?"

"I am now." Janet pulled off her T-shirt and slid into bed. Her body was stiff on the far side of the bed.

"Where were you?"

"I had to make a call."

Glancing over at the clock Sallie Lee wondered aloud, "Who on earth did you call at this hour?"

"I left a message for that doctor Ida recommended."

"I'm proud of you." Sallie Lee gazed at the tense form and hesitated for a moment. "What can I do, baby?"

"Could you hold me...please?"

Sallie Lee folded herself around her, her body meltingly warm. "You never have to ask me to hold you," she whispered into the ear near her lips. "Only to let you go."

Lifting her head slightly, she peered at Sallie Lee in the light of the moon shining into the bedroom. "You could let me go?"

"It would break my heart." Sallie Lee's voice was hoarse. "But I would never keep you where you don't want to be. My love isn't a cage."

"I know that." Janet sniffed, tears scalding her cheeks. "I was behind walls and bars for long enough to know the difference."

"Not literally, sweetheart. I meant that I want the best for you and for you to become the person you were supposed to be."

"I don't know what I want or who I am."

Sallie Lee rocked her for a few moments. "My love is big enough to let you be whoever you want to be."

"I love you." Janet glanced up. "You'll be here when I wake up?"

"In the morning and for the rest of our lives, God willing." She squeezed her lover tight and kissed her on the temple. "Now, try to sleep."

**Publications from
Bella Books, Inc.**
Women. Books. Even Better Together.
**P.O. Box 10543
Tallahassee, FL 32302
Phone: 800-729-4992
www.bellabooks.com**

CALM BEFORE THE STORM by Peggy J. Herring. Colonel Marcel Robicheaux doesn't tell and so far no one official has asked, but the amorous pursuit by Jordan McGowen has her worried for both her career and her honor.
978-0-9677753-1-9

THE WILD ONE by Lyn Denison. Rachel Weston is busy keeping home and head together after the death of her husband. Her kids need her and what she doesn't need is the confusion that Quinn Farrelly creates in her body and heart.
978-0-9677753-4-0

LESSONS IN MURDER by Claire McNab. There's a corpse in the school with a neat hole in the head and a Black & Decker drill alongside. Which teacher should Inspector Carol Ashton suspect? Unfortunately, the alluring Sybil Quade is at the top of the list. First in this highly lauded series.
978-1-931513-65-4

WHEN AN ECHO RETURNS by Linda Kay Silva. The bayou where Echo Branson found her sanity has been swept clean by a hurricane—or at least they thought. Then an evil washed up by the storm comes looking for them all, one-by-one. Second in series.
978-1-59493-225-0

DEADLY INTERSECTIONS by Ann Roberts. Everyone is lying, including her own father and her girlfriend. Leaving matters to the professionals is supposed to be easier! Third in series with *PAID IN FULL* and *WHITE OFFERINGS*.
978-1-59493-224-3

SUBSTITUTE FOR LOVE by Karin Kallmaker. No substitutes, ever again! But then Holly's heart, body and soul are captured by Reyna... Reyna with no last name and a secret life that hides a terrible bargain, one written in family blood.
978-1-931513-62-3

MAKING UP FOR LOST TIME by Karin Kallmaker. Take one Next Home Network Star and add one Little White Lie to equal mayhem in little Mendocino and a recipe for sizzling romance. This lighthearted, steamy story is a feast for the senses in a kitchen that is way too hot.
978-1-931513-61-6

2ND FIDDLE by Kate Calloway. Cassidy James's first case left her with a broken heart. At least this new case is fighting the good fight, and she can throw all her passion and energy into it.
978-1-59493-200-7

HUNTING THE WITCH by Ellen Hart. The woman she loves — used to love — offers her help, and Jane Lawless finds it hard to say no. She needs TLC for recent injuries and who better than a doctor? But Julia's jittery demeanor awakens Jane's curiosity. And Jane has never been able to resist a mystery. #9 in series and Lammy-winner.
978-1-59493-206-9

FAÇADES by Alex Marcoux. Everything Anastasia ever wanted — she has it. Sidney is the woman who helped her get it. But keeping it will require a price — the unnamed passion that simmers between them.
978-1-59493-239-7

ELENA UNDONE by Nicole Conn. The risks. The passion. The devastating choices. The ultimate rewards. Nicole Conn rocked the lesbian cinema world with *Claire of the Moon* and has rocked it again with *Elena Undone*. This is the book that tells it all...
978-1-59493-254-0

WHISPERS IN THE WIND by Frankie J. Jones. It began as a camping trip, then a simple hike. Dixon Hayes and Elizabeth Colter uncover an intriguing cave on their hike, changing their world, perhaps irrevocably.
978-1-59493-037-9

WEDDING BELL BLUES by Julia Watts. She'll do anything to save what's left of her family. Anything. It didn't seem like a bad plan...at first. Hailed by readers as Lammy-winner Julia Watts' funniest novel.
978-1-59493-199-4

WILDFIRE by Lynn James. From the moment botanist Devon McKinney meets ranger Elaine Thomas the chemistry is undeniable. Sharing—and protecting—a mountain for the length of their short assignments leads to unexpected passion in this sizzling romance by newcomer Lynn James.
978-1-59493-191-8

LEAVING L.A. by Kate Christie. Eleanor Chapin is on the way to the rest of her life when Tessa Flanagan offers her a lucrative summer job caring for Tessa's daughter Laya. It's only temporary and everyone expects Eleanor to be leaving L.A...
978-1-59493-221-2

SOMETHING TO BELIEVE by Robbi McCoy. When Lauren and Cassie meet on a once-in-a-lifetime river journey through China their feelings are innocent...at first. Ten years later, nothing—and everything—has changed. From Golden Crown winner Robbi McCoy.
978-1-59493-214-4

DEVIL'S ROCK by Gerri Hill. Deputy Andrea Sullivan and Agent Cameron Ross vow to bring a killer to justice. The killer has other plans. Gerri Hill pens another intriguing blend of mystery and romance in this page-turning thriller.
978-1-59493-218-2

SHADOW POINT by Amy Briant. Madison McPeake has just been not-quite fired, told her brother is dead and discovered she has to pick up a five-year old niece she's never met. After she makes it to Shadow Point it seems like someone—or something—doesn't want her to leave. Romance sizzles in this ghost story from Amy Briant.
978-1-59493-216-8

JUKEBOX by Gina Daggett. Debutantes in love. With each other. Two young women chafe at the constraints of parents and society with a friendship that could be more, if they can break free. Gina Daggett is best known as "Lipstick" of the columnist duo Lipstick & Dipstick.
978-1-59493-212-0

BLIND BET by Tracey Richardson. The stakes are high when Ellen Turcotte and Courtney Langford meet at the blackjack tables. Lady Luck has been smiling on Courtney but Ellen is a wild card she may not be able to handle.
978-1-59493-211-3